DR. HANDSOME

BY
NAE T. BLOSS

Dr. Handsome

Copyright © 2018 Nae T. Bloss

Chapter One

Marissa

I let out a deep sigh as I stare aimlessly into the distance twirling my straw around with my tongue. Watching as he lifts the 50-pound weight up and down over his head focusing in on the sweat dripping down his bicep. He's so perfect, his hair, his body, and the way that his lip curves to one side when he smiles is so sexy.

"Marissa, what are you doing?" Asks my sister while snapping her fingers in front of my face. "Hello, snap out of it."

"Hmm…what?" I reply adjusting myself in my chair and turning my attention to her.

She looks over her shoulder through the glass window and giggles before turning back to me. "My gosh, why don't you just go over and talk to him."

"And look like some desperate stalker. No, thank you!" I reply folding my arms across my chest.

I'd decided not to make a fool of myself and only watch from a distance. Besides once you tell a man that you're a single mother of two, that usually sends them running for the hills plus I'm pretty sure that I'm not his type. He looks as though he takes great pride in himself. Just looking at him sends a tingle down my spine and straight to the sweet spot between my thighs. 6'1, tan complexion, dirty blonde dreads, greenish

1

hazel eyes, muscular frame, and from the imprint in the front of his shorts I'd say he's packing a good 9 inches.

As for me, well I look like I've been run over twice by a semi-truck and left for dead. My looks had really become less of a priority and so had my weight. Well at least up until a couple of months ago that is. When I decided that I'd had enough of rocking the sweatpants and looking run down. I tried to put on a pair of jeans I'd bought six months ago, and I couldn't even get them past my knees. That was the first time in a while that I noticed myself. I very rarely pay attention to how I look, but that day as I stood staring in the mirror I knew I needed to wake up and get out of the rut that I was allowing myself to be stuck in.

I look up just in time to see my sister walking towards Mr. Handsome and it pulls my focus back to the present.

"Omg, what is she doing?" I say to myself sinking into my chair in a panic.

She stops in front of him and extends her hand out to him, he sits down the weight and shakes her hand. They talk for a few minutes then she turns and points in my direction, his gaze follows her hand and he looks over at me flashing a huge grin my way. At that moment all I could think was once she returned I was going to give her a mouth full. They shake hands once more and she turns to head back over to the table or, so I thought. Instead, she gives me a sneaky grin then turns down the hall towards the locker room waving as she disappears.

I look back in his direction and I see him get up from the bench, grab a towel, and begin walking towards me. I wanted to get up and run away but my legs wouldn't allow me to stand. My heart began pounding into my chest, my hands, along with other parts of my body began to sweat and it felt like someone switched off the A/C and cut on the heat.

"Hello, it's Marissa, right?"

I try to speak but the words wouldn't come out, I sat gawking at him like some insane person. He smiles at me as he pulls up a chair and takes a seat. My mouth was dry, so I pick up my smoothie and take a sip then straighten myself in my seat.

"Hi, yes, it's Marissa."

"Beautiful name. It's nice to meet you."

"Thanks!" I say with a shy smile, pushing a loose strand of hair behind my ear. "Oh—um, I'm sorry about before, I was a little caught off guard."

"It's all good, no need to apologize. I was just coming over to introduce myself, my name is Brendan."

"Nice to meet you, Brendan."

"Can I get you a fresh one?" He asks nodding towards my cup.

I nod yes, and he gets up from his seat and heads over to the smoothie bar to grab us fresh drinks. He glances back at me with a huge grin on his face as he walks away as if he could feel my gaze following him.

A few seconds later he returns and reclaims his seat sliding the cup over to me.

"Here you go, one berry passion smoothie for the lady."

"Thanks," I said reaching over and quickly picking up the cup.

I've never tried any of the passion drinks before, but it was delicious. I guess I'll have to add it to my list of favs. I watch him place the straw in between his lips as his eyes connect with mine and my heart begins to race once again. How can he get my blood rushing with just one look? I lower my eyes to his lips, the sexiest set of lips that I've ever seen on a man in my life. He takes another sip and lets the straw slowly slide from between them and then licks his lips again, slow and seductively biting his lower lip. My lady pearl tingled between my thighs as I thought of how it would feel to have his mouth pressed against my swollen lips as his tongue slides between them thrusting my clit.

"So, your sister tells me that you have a little crush on me. Is that true?" He asks, smiling over at me continuing to bite his bottom lip after noticing my reaction.

My eyes grow wide and I try to give him a flirty smile, but a nervous giggle comes out instead, "I—um, I don't know why she said that. I mean don't get me wrong, I do find you very attractive." I say realizing that I was babbling so I just stopped talking.

A wide smile spreads across his face, "Well thank you. And I find you to be very beautiful as well." He says and leans forward. "How about you take my number and give me a call later so that we can continue our conversation." I stretch out my hand to him and he writes his number on the palm of my hand. "I hope to hear from you soon," he says winking at me before getting up from his seat and walking away.

I exhale the breath that I'd been holding in as he was touching my hand. Once he was gone I got up from my seat and headed towards the locker room in search of my sister. I walk to our lockers and find Natalie sitting on the bench with her towel wrapped around her, she'd already showered and was applying lotion to her legs.

"Are you insane? Ugh, I could really choke the life out of you right now."

She looks up and smiles at me then continues putting on her lotion. "So, when's the wedding?" She asks sarcastically as she giggled.

"That's not funny, Natalie, you put me on the spot."

"Pssh... you'll get over it. So, did you get his number?" She said, brushing off the fact that I was serious.

"Yes," I reply leaning up against the locker, rolling my eyes at her, and crossing my arms over my chest.

"Good! Well, in that case, you can thank me by buying me lunch. Now go get dressed so we can go." She said, standing up and removing her towel.

"Ugh... seriously!" I say with a huff then turn and walk away.

I head into the shower and then get dressed. I head outside to meet my sister at the car, as I make my way through the parking lot I see my sister leaned up against the car flirting with some random guy. He looks like one of those men that are into heavy metal or rock judging from the way he was dressed.

"Ewe," I shake my head in disgust, walk over to the driver's side, and open the door.

"Hey sis, are you ready to go?" she asks quickly throwing her cigarette to the ground, but it was too late I'd already seen her.

"That's going to kill you, you know," I say sternly as I get into the car.

She taps the screen on her phone and then says bye to the guy and hops in the car. I pull out of the parking space and head towards the street.

"So, when are you going to call him?" She asks, breaking the silence.

"Why?"

"Um, let's see perhaps because you haven't gotten laid in two years. And trust me, if you want me to keep my sanity I'm a need you to get some dick in your life." She says giving me a side eye and shifting in her seat. "Seriously, your kind of cranky these days and honestly, it's throwing you off your game sis. I mean look at you do you even care about how you look anymore? And I'd hate to see what your juice box looks like right now."

"Aw sis, I didn't know you cared so much about my juice box," I say sarcastically, pouting my lips out at her and she gives me the finger.

****

I wake up to the sound of kids running through the house screaming at the top of their lungs. I roll over onto my back and blow my hair out of my face.

"Quiet down out there," I yell to the two of them.

My son runs into the room and leaps onto the bed. "Yay, mommy's awake," he says as he continues to jump on the bed.

6

I reach up, grab him, and toss him on the bed tickling him as he laughs hysterically. My daughter burst around the corner and into the room.

"Tickle time with mommy," she screams as she jumps on the bed laughing, joining in with me and her brother.

We roll around the bed tickling each other for a while then I notice the time. "Come on you guys, let's go get some breakfast," I say, and they bounce off the bed and onto their feet disappear out the room.

I take a second and sit up on the side of the bed gathering my thoughts before heading down to the kitchen. I whip up some scrambled eggs, bacon, and heart shaped pancakes for the kiddos then grab a cup of coffee for myself, trying to perk myself up as they finish their breakfast.

This was usually my husband's thing, making breakfast for the family. He'd passed away two years ago in a car accident and the kids and I miss him a great deal. He would always wake up early, cook breakfast for all of us, then get the kids off to school while I got ready for work. I can still picture him at the table laughing and joking with the children, bouncing our daughter on his knee as she sang "I'm a little princess" repeatedly.

"Hey mom, are you ok?" my son asks, bringing my mind back to the present as he handed me his plate. I take the plate and quickly walk over to the sink blinking away the tears that started to fill my eyes, "Yes, baby, I'm ok. You and your sister go and finish getting ready for school." I say turning to him and offering him a reassuring smile. I gather the rest of the dishes and clean up the little spills before they make their way back.

I sit out on the front steps with them waiting for the school bus to arrive. It was only the second week of school and the kids were still excited as if it was still the first day. Josh is now in the third grade and my little princess Jasmine is in the 1st grade. It still amazes me how quickly they've grown up.

The bus arrives and Jasmine hugs me before she leaps off the porch and runs to the end of the sidewalk. My son kisses my cheek and gives me a fist bump before walking out to the bus. I wave to the bus driver and once again to my children as the bus pulls off and disappears into the distances. I walk back inside and close the door behind me leaning back on it for a moment before heading back up to my room and throwing myself onto the bed. Several weeks had gone by and I still hadn't gathered up enough nerve to call Mr. Handsome and by now he's probably forgotten all about me.

I go into my walk-in closet and take out a pair of yoga pants and a white tank top. I've been working out a lot lately, so I was starting to feel like the old me again. I shower quickly, then dress, I throw my hair in a messy bun then walk over to the big mirror and give myself a once-over. Wow, my body had really bounced back in a major way.

"Mama's still got it," I say as I twist my hips then turn to check out the back side. Oh my, those 50 squats, twice a day have done wonders. I grab my phone off the nightstand and snap a couple of pictures then head downstairs. I grab my purse and keys then head out the door.

Sliding into the driver's seat of my BMW I place my purse in the passenger's seat and start the car. I connect my phone to the Bluetooth then press the call button and listen to the line ring for what seemed like ages and finally after the fourth ring I get an answer.

"Hello," I hear his sexy baritone speak over the line.

"Hi, Brendan, this is Marissa. We met at the other day at the gym." I say, my voice cracking a little.

"Hello, Marissa, I've been waiting for your call. How are you?"

"I'm great. Um, so I was calling to see if maybe you'd like to meet me for coffee or maybe lunch this afternoon."

"Sure, I would love to. Where would you like to meet?" He said, and I could hear the smile in his voice.

"How about Sal's, at say 12:30 pm?"

"Of course, that sounds good to me. I'll see you there."

I end the call and take a deep breath then slowly exhale. "Omg, I have a lunch date with Mr. Handsome," I shout as I squirm around in my seat, clapping my hands, and swinging my head back and forth.

After a couple of minutes, I regain my composure and pull out of the driveway and head downtown. I have a couple of hours, so I head to the nail salon and get a Mani & Pedi, then head over to the hair salon to see if my hair stylist can squeeze me in. I haven't been to the salon in such a long time, so I know I'm well overdue for a trim.

After an hour in my stylist's chair, my hair was back to perfection and my make-up beat to the gods, as my hair stylist says. I hug her and say goodbye then head home to change into something a little more appealing.

I pull on a pair of skinny jeans and a cute little red tunic top and a pair of tan wedges. I pull my hair into a neat bun, touch up my make-up, and check myself in the mirror once more before heading out. I make it to the restaurant 10 minutes early, so I sit in the car getting myself together and going over some questions in my mind that I wanted to ask, as well as my answers to the things I think he might ask me. When the clock read 12:25 pm I headed inside the restaurant were a tall and slender brunette greeted me with a welcoming smile.

"Hello, welcome to Sal's. How many will we be seating today?" She asks, her voice energetic.

"A table for two, please." I hear a deep voice say from behind me.

I turn back and see Brendan as he walks up behind me, he kisses me on the cheek and places his hand on the small of my back.

"Hello lovely," he whispers into my ear and it sends a tingle down my spine.

She seats us at our table and hands us our menus letting us know that our waitress will be with us momentarily before walking away.

"Wow, I feel a little underdressed," I say admiring his designer suit.

He laughs, as he takes off his jacket placing it on the back of the chair and adjusts his tie. "Oh, don't mind me I came straight here from my office. And you look stunning might I add."

"Thanks," I say feeling the heat rush to my face. "May I ask what your profession is?"

"I don't know," he said. "Is this a date?" he asks with his eyebrow furred.

"Um I—I"

"I mean I don't feel inclined to go to deep into my personal life unless this is in fact a date." He smirks.

I look away and began fiddled with the napkin that I'd placed in my lap as a brief silence lingers before he leans forward and says my name. The way that he said my name sent chills down my spine and I wanted to hear him say it over and over again.

"I'm sorry," I say clearing my throat. "Would you call this a date?" I ask, countering his question.

"Sure, I could see this as a first of many dates."

"Well there you have it," I say in a soft voice.

The waitress walks over to the table just as he was about to continue and asks if we're ready to order. He orders a steak medium rare with a side of mashed potatoes and asparagus which sounded good, so I told her that I'd have the same. She took our menus then scurried off to the back to put in our order.

"I'm a doctor," he continues, "I have my own practice on the upper west side of town.

"Doctor. Mm, I'm sure the ladies have no complaints when they enter the room and see you standing there." I say raising one eyebrow.

He chuckles. "And what is it that you do lovely?"

"I own a restaurant," I said, pausing for a brief second before continuing. "Well, my late husband and I both started the business. But he passed away a couple of years ago, in a car accident."

11

His gaze meets mine and I could see the compassion in his eyes, "Oh, I'm sorry to hear that."

The waitress returns to the table with our food and I was kind of glad she did because I wasn't too sure if I could handle finishing this particular conversation. We dove right into eating our meal while continuing our conversation. In the hour that we dined I learned that he is 33, single, no children, never married, and is also a well-renowned surgeon. His openness made me a little curious as to why such a wonderful man such as himself has never married. He seems like the perfect guy from where I'm sitting.

By the time we finished dessert, he had explained to me that he had come close, once. He was madly in love with his ex-fiancé whom he thought he'd be with forever. But, it turns out she couldn't handle his long hours and demanding schedule.

The time we spent together was wonderful and the conversation was effortless, and I really like that. After we finished our meal he paid the bill then walked me out to my car, opening the door for me once I pressed the button for the lock then I slid inside.

"Well, I had an amazing time." He said, "Maybe, if you're not too busy, we could go to dinner next week, and you could bring your kids along.

As much as I like him I don't think that I'm ready for him to meet my kids just yet. I was still sensitive to the fact that they've only seen me with one man and that was their father and I'd never really thought about sitting them down and talking to them about it. But then again, I didn't think that I would be dating again and look how that turned out.

"Mm… Let me think about it." I replied not wanting to give him a solid no.

"Of course," He said, with a warm smile then leans in and kisses me on the cheek before closing my door. He steps back from the car and waves to me as I pull out of the driveway and into the afternoon traffic.

Chapter Two

Brendan

I stand there in the parking lot waving like some love-sick puppy as she drove away then turned and headed to my Mercedes that was parked on the opposite side of the restaurant.

I'm no stranger to beautiful women swooning over me and being that I haven't been a one-woman man since my ex-walked out on me several years ago, I don't mind. But I can say that there is something different about this one, something that intrigues me, and it wasn't like I hadn't noticed the looks she had given me at the gym and I can all but imagine the dirty things that were running through her mind.

Even during lunch, I could see the lust in her eyes, the longing, and the need to be pleasured. She'd said that her husband had passed away two years ago and from the way she shut down when we began to talk about it I was sure that she hadn't been with anyone since. And on top of that, she has two young children at home, so there's surely no one-night stands creeping in and out before the sunrises.

"Welcome back Dr. Hopkins," Janice said. "How was your lunch date?"

"It was only lunch; Janice and it went well. I like her." I said, with a cunning smile.

"Oh, do tell?" She said turning in her chair than standing and following me back into my office.

14

Janice was like a second mother to me and a bit pushy when it came to my love life. So, I knew that she wasn't going to let up or let me get back to my appointments. At least not until I gave her every detail of my afternoon with Marissa.

"There isn't much to tell really her name is Marissa, she's 28 years old, she has two kids, and she owns her own business, a restaurant," I said, glancing up to catch the look on her face after I mentioned the word kids.

She placed her hand on her hip and raised an eyebrow waiting for me to continue but I remained silent. So, she walked over to the chair in front of my desk and sat down crossing her legs and staring at me with prying eyes.

"What?" I ask, setting my pen down on the notepad and leaning back in my seat.

"Kids?" She said shocked. "She has two kids?"

"Yes. She was happily married for 10 years but her husband died in a car accident a couple of years ago."

"Oh, my, that poor thing." She gasps placing her hand on her chest. "Sweetheart, listen, I want you to get back out there and find someone, but do you really think that you're ready for someone with that kind of emotional scarring?"

I look at her with a sideways glance. "Of course, or I'm at least willing to give it a try."

"And two children. Are you sure you're ready to take that on as well?" She asks with a serious expression on her face.

I lean forward and rest my arms on my desk. "What are you trying to say, Janice?"

She paused for a moment and looked out of the window beside her before turning her attention back to me.

"I just want you to really think about it before you pursue this young woman. There is no uncomplicated way to walk away from a relationship like this once you've gotten in too deep, and it's not only her there are two young children that hang in the balance. So, if you're just planning on getting close to this young woman just to shoot off a few jizzes, then don't."

I remain quiet taking in all that she'd said, and I understood where she was coming from. What if we did start dating and things went sour between the two of us, I wouldn't only be hurting her once I walked away I would hurt those two innocent little kids as well. I let out a long sigh then looked over to Janice who was patiently waiting for me to respond.

"I hear what you're saying but let's not jump the gun. We've only had lunch together and there was no jizzing involved. So, let's wait until at least the third date before you go getting all deep on me, ok." I say offering her a small smile.

"You're right." She said standing up, straightening her blouse, and smoothing out her skirt. "When the time comes I suppose we will revisit this conversation, but for now you have patients young man, so you better get a move on." She winks at me and heads out the door closing it halfway.

I open my laptop and pull up my emails. I have about 15 minutes before my next appointment, so I'll try and view a few emails before they show up. But just as luck would have it as soon as I pull up the browser and began to click the first email on my list there's a knock at the door.

16

"Dr. Hopkins, I'm sorry to bother you but your new patient is here early." The nurse says peeking her head around the door.

I let out a sigh and close my laptop before getting up and walking over to grab my coat. I take the folder from her then follow alongside her as we walk down the hall to the exam room. I look over the information for the patient, a Mr. Pedregon, before entering the room. I tap on the door lightly then open it and go inside.

"Good afternoon, Mr. Pedregon?" I say in the form of a question as I pronounce his last name.

"Yes, sir, that'd be me." He says with a bit of a country accent and I could tell immediately that he was new to the city.

"Alright, well let's get started. What brings you in today?" I ask sitting on the stool and crossing one leg over the other resting the folder on my lap.

I found it quite humbling that I was the first doctor that came to mind when patients ask about recommendations for the best doctors in the state of Tennessee. I listened intently as he explained to me some of the problems that he'd been having the past several weeks. He also mentioned that his wife had been on him about going to see a professional, so that's what brought him in today.

I jotted a few things down on my sheet then I gave him a full exam. He was in his late thirties, and he was also very healthy, but still too young to be having some of the pains that he'd described to me.

"Mr. Pedregon, what is it that you do for a living?"

17

"I own a construction company."

And just like that, I knew what was causing the pains that he was having. I explain to him that for a lot of construction workers, their bodies take a daily beating as far as all the heavy lifting, standing for extended periods of time, and having to bend and move in all types of spaces can cause strain on the joints and muscles.

I offer a few different solutions then I turn to write another little note on my sheet when there's a soft knock at the door. I call out for them to come in and I hear the door open and I see him motioning someone into the room.

"Come on in darling," he said, "We're just finishing up."

"Great, I had the hardest time finding a parking spot." The lady said.

My heart stopped, and my body went numb as I listened to the voice that seemed to echo in the room. I put down my pen and slowly turned around, I couldn't believe my eyes, it was her, standing just a couple of inches from me. She looked up at me and the smile on her face faded and her breath caught in her throat as she stared at me with eyes wide.

"Brendan," she managed to say her voice cracking.

I swallow hard trying to get the lump that was stuck in my throat out before speaking. "Nia," I finally said, but my voice failed me and cracked a little.

"Um doc—sweetheart," He said looking back and forth between the two of us. "Do you all know each other?" He asks as the room went quiet again.

Finally, she broke the silence walking over and placing her hand on his shoulder moving her other up and down his arm then clearing her throat before she began.

"Honey, do you remember me telling you about my ex-fiancé. The one that I'd said was a brilliant doctor."

"Yes," he says nodding then he shoots up straight, it was like a light bulb went off in his head and he turned and looked at me. "Oh, so the doc here is your ex. Well, I'll be damned what are the odds of that." He says with a loud gut-busting laugh.

Nia and I look at each other and she has an embarrassment look on her face and her husband's horrible banter wasn't making it any better. She looks away from me as her cheeks become rosy red and her eyes fill with tears.

"Will you excuse me for a second, Mr. Pedregon?" I say picking up the folder and leaving the room.

As I start down the hall Nia steps out of the room calling out my name as she rushs to catch up with me. I don't turn around or answer her and when she finally catches up to me I feel her hand on my arm and I freeze.

"Brendan, please, wait a second." She says out of breath from the run.

I ignore her pulling my arm away and walk into my office. I stand by the window looking out onto the busy streets I close my eyes and take a deep breath as she continues to try and get my attention once again.

"I'm sorry, I—I didn't know that this was your practice. If I'd known I would never have—" She pauses, and I turn to meet her gaze.

19

"Why?" I ask, my voice a low growl.

She looks away from me her gaze dropping to the floor as if she's searching for the answer to my question. A drawn-out silence hung in the balance for several moments before I walk over and take the seat in front of my desk then offer her the one beside me. She'd hurt me, broken my heart even, but I wasn't going to let my emotions get the best of me and be an asshole to her even though she deserves it.

"I'm sorry Brendan," she says finally breaking the silence.

"You just left. Why?"

She'd packed her things and left the home we shared while I was working late at the hospital one night. I'd come home the next morning to a note on the table in the foyer and after that, I never saw her again not until now a year and a half later. I was hurt by the fact that she didn't even have the guts to tell me to my face and yes, I'd known that there were things that she wanted from our relationship that I wasn't interested in but to just leave with no explanation after all those years together, I at least deserved that much.

"I was afraid, and I didn't really know how to say it to you. I told myself that I was going to sit down with you once you were home and let you know that I'd been seeing someone else, but the more I thought about your reaction and the painful look, like the one you have right now, and I freaked out. So, I just packed my things and left you the note. I figured it would be easier that way."

"It wasn't," I say cutting her off. "Seven years together Nia and you just walked out on me. You should've told me what you were feeling or at least let me know that you were slipping away from me. I would've done anything for you,

20

you were my entire world and you just threw it all away in one night."

She moved closer to me placing her hand on my arm, but I moved it away quickly. She slowly moved her hand away and I could see the hurt look in her eyes. I didn't want to make her feel bad, but I couldn't handle feeling the touch of her hand on me it was too much.

She stood from her seat and walked towards the door pausing to look back at me, "I'm really sorry, Brendan. I hope that you can forgive me," she says then turns and leaves my office.

The numbed feelings were back and all the old wounds that I'd thought had healed felt fresh once again, and I couldn't bring myself to move from the chair. I leaned forward in my seat and placed my hands over my face taking slow steady breaths.

"Dr. Hopkins," the nurse calls out my name her voice soft as she steps into my office. "Would you like for me to finish up with Mr. Pedregon?"

I sit up straight and look over at her, she had a look of concern on her face as she studied my expression. "Yes, please," I say with a small smile. "I've written everything there in his file and let him know that we will be calling in two prescriptions that he can pick up at his pharmacy tomorrow morning," I reply trying to keep my voice calm and professional and she nods her head and grabs the folder from my desk before heading out of my office.

****

By the end of the day, I'd pulled myself together and gotten back to work finishing up with the rest of my patient. I was happy when 6 PM rolled around and the day was finally done. Janice and I were the last two in the office she was finishing up some paperwork and I was responding to the last couple of emails.

At around 6:45 pm Janice peeked into my office with a huge grin on her face. "Hey, I'm heading out you care to join me?" she asks pulling on her jacket.

"Not tonight Janice, but thanks for the offer," I said offering her a weak smile and she returns a closed lip smile before saying goodnight.

Once I hear the door close I lean back into my chair and let out a heavy sigh. I was confused by what I was feeling, and I didn't know how to handle it. Seeing Nia again brought back so many memories as well as the pain that I'd felt the last couple of years after she'd left, but besides all of that I still felt love for this woman. I wasn't completely over her, but our conversation did give me a bit of closure and I could see the pain and guilt in her eyes, so I knew that she was genuinely sorry for walking away from me the way she did.

And it was clear that she'd move on from the past and married. My heart ached at the thought of her moving on so quickly and finding another man to take my place in her heart.

My phone buzzed, and I reached over and flipped it so that I could see the screen. It was a message from Marissa and for the first time today my lips pulled into a smile and I was elated to hear from her so soon. She thanked me for meeting her for lunch this afternoon and I typed out a short reply and pressed send.

Ten minutes later I pressed send on my last email, closed my laptop, and scooted away from my desk. I grab my jacket and my briefcase then head out the door into the cool night air. I get into my car and pull onto the empty street. I wasn't in the mood to go and sit at home alone, so I headed to the bar that my staff and I usually go to after a long week. But tonight, I'm flying solo and hoping that a couple of drinks can ease my mind.

Chapter Three

Marissa

I close my eyes and massage my temples. Tonight's been stressful, we were overcrowded, and someone on my staff booked two parties for tonight that ended up being too close together.

I pull myself together and take a couple of painkillers before going out to greet the customers and see how everyone is enjoying their meals. Also, to make sure that my staff is meeting all their expectations. As I walk over to my last table, I notice a man sitting alone in the corner of the restaurant. Once I get closer to him I recognize Brendan's face and my heart skips a beat.

"Well, this is a surprise," I said, walking up to the table. "How did you know this was my restaurant?"

"I didn't." He said with a chuckle, gazing at me with a surprised look on his face. "I was having dinner with a few of my colleagues and they chose this place for dinner, they just headed out."

"Oh… I see." I say as disappointment swept over me.

"Come, sit down and join me, you look like you need a break." He says with a grin. "You have quite the place here and the food is incredible."

"Thanks," I say as I slide into the seat beside him.

The conversation was easy and carefree the same as the other day when we had lunch. A couple of hours pass, and the restaurant begins to clear out, but we hadn't noticed. We were so wrapped up in one another that nothing or anyone else in the room really mattered. I was really enjoying this time, it'd been so long since I'd felt connected and in tune with any man other than my husband and it actually kind of scares me.

I sometimes ask myself will I ever really be able to give my whole heart to someone else? Can I allow myself to ever truly fall in love again? Only time will tell and who knows maybe this gorgeous man in front of me will turn out to be the one that captures my heart.

****

The kids and I decide to visit my mother and father for the day since my daughter told me that she was overdue for a playdate with grandpa. After gathering a few things for the ride, we climb into the car and head over to my parents' house in Brentwood.

"Grandma," Josh said, jumping out of the car and running into her arms.

"There's my big boy." She said planting kisses all over his face leaving behind smeared lipstick.

"Grandma, Grandma," Jasmine screamed running a couple of steps behind her brother.

"Hello, my Princess." My mother says scooping her into her arms then turns to me. "Hello sweetheart, I'm so happy you all stopped by." She said, wiping the lipstick from Jasmine's cheek.

"Hi, mom," I said kissing her cheek. "Princess Jasmine here wanted to see her grandpa," I say rubbing the top of her head,

25

but she shakes her head for me to stop while giving us a big and bright beautiful smile.

I can see her father in her every time she smiles. She favors him so much more than me and she also has his easygoing personality. My mother places her back on her feet and she darts towards the house, opening the front door, and running inside in search of my father.

We go inside and I help my mother prepare dinner while the kids play in the den with my dad. It's been awhile since we've had Sunday dinner with my parents and I have to admit I miss being in the kitchen with my mother dancing around to the tunes of Frank Sinatra.

"So, your sister tells me that you're seeing someone."

I roll my eyes and sigh loudly. "When will she learn to stay out of my personal life," I say bearing down hard as I slice the tomato.

"So, what's his name and what does he do for a living?" She asks, turning and facing me with one hand on her hip leaning against the counter.

"First of all were not dating," I say giving my mother a side glance. "And his name is Dr. Brendan Hopkins, we met at the gym."

"Oh, a doctor." She says in a playful voice shaking her shoulders.

I ignore her and continue chopping the rest of the vegetables for the salad and place them in a bowl while listening to my mother begin her list of 21 questions. I should have known that my sister would call our mom and blab about me and Brendan, my sister's mouth is like running water.

The kids help my mother and I set the table as my dad brings out the food and arranges it on the table. We all take our seats and reach out, taking each other's hands, and bow our heads as my father says grace. We sit quietly enjoying dinner, the kids love my mother's meatloaf, it's actually the one thing they have no problem scarfing down and doing it quietly.

"So, how's everything going with the restaurant sweetheart?" My father asks before scooping up a spoonful of mashed potatoes.

"It's great, business has picked up a lot more here lately."

"That's great honey. I'm glad that you stuck with it."

"Me too dad," I reply offering him a small smile.

A couple of months after Chandler died the restaurant took a major hit financially and I didn't think that we would be able to bounce back from it. My dad had offered to loan me the money I needed to keep it afloat, but I was determined to fix things on my own. So, I got a loan from the bank, remodeled a little, made some changes to the menu, and then we began booking parties and having kid's nights. Before I knew it, business was booming, and things were getting back to normal.

I help my mom with the dishes after dinner and once everything was all cleaned up my dad helped me out to the car. He looked like macho man carrying both my son and daughter in his arms as they rested their head on each shoulder sound asleep. He places them in the car and gets them safely buckled in then closes the door and hugs me tight kissing my cheek before I turn to slide into the driver seat. He watches as I pull out of the driveway and waves one last time before heading back inside.

I drive home with the music playing low so that it doesn't wake them. My phone buzzes, and I quickly press the end call button sending it to voicemail rather than picking it up and having it come through the speakers and waking the kids. I will check it once I'm home and the kids are in bed.

I didn't really want to wake my son but getting them both in the house would be hard. One inside I tuck them into bed and head downstairs to the kitchen to grab a bottle of wine from the fridge. I pour myself a glass then head into the living room to get comfortable on the sofa. This has always been my time to relax and enjoy some me time and trust me by the end of the day it is much needed.

Remembering the call that I'd gotten in the car earlier I reach over and pick up my phone to scroll through my missed calls. I had two from my sister, but I wasn't too worried about calling her back after she blabbed to our mom about Dr. Handsome. And then there was one missed call from Brendan.

My breath catches as I sit up straight up on the sofa. My stomach turns flips as I sit staring at his name on the screen, I glance up at the time and it's a little after nine.

"That's not too late to call back, right?" I ask myself contemplating whether or not I should wait until morning.

It's early, but it's also a Sunday night so maybe he's getting ready to turn in. No, it's too early for that as well. Besides he doesn't look like the type that goes to bed this early at night then again, he doesn't look like the type that would be alone on a Sunday night either. I glance at the phone again for a second then shake the last thought from my head and press the call button and quickly place the phone to my ear.

I could always hang up or if he sounds like he's asleep I'll apologize and call him back tomorrow.

"Hello," he said, his voice low and husky sending goosebumps over my body.

"Hi, um it's Marissa," I say my voice shaky as my nerves kick in.

His voice makes the space between my thighs ache every time I hear it and when he says my name I melt as my body fills with desire.

"Yes, how are you?"

"I'm good, I was just returning your call from earlier this evening," I say then smack myself on the forehead after I say it. I was making things awkward and I sound like I'm calling back a client rather than a guy I'm interested in, ugh—what is wrong with me?

"Well I hadn't heard from you in a couple of days, so I figured it was my turn to give you a call."

"How sweet you were thinking about me," I say in a playful voice.

He chuckles, "Yes, well I've actually been thinking about you a lot lately." He replies.

I was surprised. Even though our lunch had gone well, and we had a great conversation at the restaurant the other night, in the back of mind I still can't believe he's into me. I mean I'm not sure if he's just entertaining me because he thinks I need the attention or not, but a man like Brendan can get any woman he wants, definitely someone much hotter than me.

"Are you still there?" He says, and I focus my attention back on the call.

"Yeah, sorry,"

"If you're unable to talk I completely understand. I'm sure it's your kids bedtime and you're probably handling that right now."

"No, they are already in bed." I blurt out in a rush not ready to end the call just yet.

"Ok," He said, and I could tell that he was smiling. "So how was your day?" he asks.

We spend the next two hours talking and by the end of the call, I had agreed to go to his place for dinner tomorrow night. Lying in bed I couldn't help but think "what have I gotten myself into?" I mean sitting down in a restaurant around other people is one thing, but being in his home just the two of us is a little more intimate.

I sigh.

I don't know if this is a good idea?

Chapter Four

Brendan

After getting off the phone with Marissa last night all I could think about was her shy and sexy little voice. It echoed in my ear over and over again. Later that night I stroked my dick as I imagined her laying in my bed, her thick chocolate thighs spread wide for me as I take her pussy into my mouth pleasuring her with my tongue. Even now my dick jumps at the thought of her moaning my name.

But tonight, I would have to get a grip and show some self-control. I want her, and I want her bad, but I don't want to push or make her feel as though I'm rushing her to jump in the sack with me. Plus, she seems to be sort of timid when it comes to being around men, and I don't want to scare her off, so for now I'll take it slow. I shake the thoughts from my mind and try to finish up the paperwork that's been piling up on my desk. Even though I know I'm not going to get everything finished in less than two hours, especially with thoughts of Marissa on the brain, I still jump right into work. An hour goes by, I finish up, and closeout my laptop then grabs my things and head out of my office.

"Leaving so soon?" Janice asks surveying me with questioning eyes?

"Uh—yeah. I have a few stops to make before I head home." I reply grabbing my things and bolting towards the door.

"I see," She says squinting her eyes as she turns and follows behind me as I walk to the front of the office. "So, your rush to dash out of here wouldn't happen to have anything to do with that beautiful young woman sitting there in the corner now would it? She was asking to speak with you, she said her name is Marissa."

I stop and look at Janice then over to the left where she was pointing and there sat Marissa with a little girl snuggled in her lap resting her head on her mother's chest. I drop my briefcase next to the reception desk and rush over to her taking the seat beside her.

"Hey, is everything ok?" I ask, a little concerned once I saw how pale the little girl looked.

"I'm sorry to just drop in like this but as you can see my little one's not feeling so well. I'd tried to make it to the pediatrician before the office closed but the traffic is terrible, so I figured I'd stop by and let you know that I'd need to cancel our date so that I can take her to the emergency room."

"There's no need for that I've seen all of my patient for the day, so I can take a quick look at her," I say placing my hand on the little girl's head to see if she felt warm. "Come with me to the back and let's find out what's going on."

"Oh no, I don't want to impose. Really I was so close that I figured why not just stop and speak with you—"

"Nonsense," I said cutting her off. "You're here, I'm a doctor, and this is the number one family practice in Tennessee, so why not?"

She looks down at the little girl and after thinking it over for a few seconds she breathes a heavy sigh then rises from her seat. She follows the nurse to the back and I gather my things and head back to my office to grab a few papers for her to fill out while I do the exam.

"Thank you for doing this," she says her eyes soft as she looks over at me.

She looked tired, but she's probably been up all night with her daughter. I offered her a small smile then took the little girl from her arms and placed her on the exam table. Her eyes flutter open and she stares up at me offering me a weak smile.

"Hi," she said her voice barely a whisper.

"Hello, sweetheart. My name is Dr. Hopkins can you tell me your name?"

"Jasmine," she said, suddenly grabbing and tugging at her tummy."

"That's a very pretty name." I reply "So, Jasmine can you show me where you are hurting."

I needed her to point to all the places that are causing her pain and she points to her throat, her stomach, and her head. I turn and look at Marissa and she nods to me letting me know that was correct then I turn my attention back to her daughter.

"Does your tummy hurt more or does your throat bother you more?"

She points to her throat and her head and I nod back at her and gently rub the top of her head. She gives me another weak smile then looks over at her mom and says.

"Will I feel better now mommy?" She asks.

"Yes princess, Dr. Hopkins is going to give you a special medicine that is just for you and it's going to make everything all better." She said giving her a comforting smile.

I write down a few things in my notes and take the paperwork from her and take it out to Janice so that she can start processing it then I join them again in the room. The nurse was just about to swab her throat when I walked back in the room and I could see that little Jasmine had a horrid look on her face, so I walk over to her and place my hand gently on her arm.

"It's ok sweetheart. Sarah just needs to tickle the back of your throat so that she can run a test and it's going to tell us what's wrong, ok," I said, my lips pulling into a smile as I try and comfort her.

"Ok, but can you hold my hand?" she asks.

"Of course," I said reaching over and taking her tiny little hand in mine then she squeezes her eyes shut and opens her mouth big and wide.

"All done," the nurse said smiling at her.

"See, now that wasn't all bad was it?" I ask, and she shakes her head as her lips pull into a small smile.

I look over at Marissa who is staring at me with a wide smile on her face and her eyes lit up.

"I believe this little princess may have streptococcal pharyngitis." I say, and she raises her eyebrow and looks up at me and I laugh. "Strep throat," I say giving her the more common name for it.

"Oh, got it." She nods. "And that causes a stomach ache?" she asks confused.

"Yes, it can and usually does in younger children," I reply taking a seat on the stool next to the exam table. "We'll know for sure once the test comes back and then I can write you a prescription that she'll need to start taking immediately because it is contagious. So, be sure to wash her bedding and use disinfectant to get rid of the germs around the house."

She nods her head and stands to her feet and walks over to her daughter and begins stroking her hair.

"Thank again for this. And I'm sorry that I had to cancel our dinner tonight."

"It's not a problem," I say, "You have more important things to take care of," I say looking from her to the little girl with a smile.

I sit in the room waiting with them and talking to her about her day. My nursing assistant appears in the doorway and lets me know that the results were positive for strep, so I write her a prescription for some antibiotics then walk her to the front door where we say our goodbyes.

I head back to my office and drop down into my chair and exhale a deep breath before picking up my phone and ordering some take out. After placing my order, I go back out to the waiting room and grab my briefcase that was still sitting where I left it and head out to my car.

I guess I'll be spending another night alone.

****

Pleasuring myself late night has now become a thing for me since Marissa came into my life. Any other time I would have stopped off at the bar and picked up a couple of females and brought them back for a rough sex session and then kicked them out before sunrise.

I get up and get dressed preparing myself for yet another long workday. I shower then put on a pair of jeans and a collared shirt since today is casual Friday at the office. I make my morning coffee and fill up my mug that the staff had gotten me for Christmas last year and head out the door. I'm surprised by how light traffic is this morning, getting to the office was a breeze, I made it a whole twenty minutes earlier than I'd expected to. None of the ladies had arrived yet so I let myself in and headed straight to my office hoping to get some paperwork done and answer a few emails before the day starts.

I place my things in the corner of my office then take a seat behind my desk and power up my laptop. I remove my phone from my bag and see that I have a voice message from Marissa, so I pull up her text and start to type out a message, but I quickly change my mind. Treating her daughter, the other night gives me a reason to call rather than sending a text message. So, I scroll through my recent calls and press her name listening as the phone springs to life and after the second ring, her shy and soft voice comes over the line.

"Hey, you," She says her voice low almost a whisper.

"Hey, did I wake you?" I ask

"No, No. I'm just looking in on Jasmine she's still sleeping."

"Good, how is she feeling?"

"She's doing so much better and the meds are working like a dream. I actually got a full night sleep, no interruptions." She said with a giggle.

Even her laugh makes my dick twitch every time I hear it and I wonder now if I make her feel the same way whenever she thinks of me. I could tell by the way she looked at me at the gym that she wanted me but now she's got me wondering just how bad. A small smile plays on my lips as I think of her perfect lips wrapped around my cock and the feel of her tongue lapping around the head of my dick while I finger her tight wet pussy.

"Hey, are you still there?" She says breaking my concentration.

"Yes, I'm here," I reply pushing the thoughts from my mind.

"I was saying thank you for seeing her and taking care of my little princess. Also, I wanted to see if perhaps we could reschedule or dinner date?"

"Sure, whenever you'd like."

"How about tomorrow night?"

"That's perfect," I say with a grin that touched each ear excitedly.

We spoke a few more words then ended the call. For the rest of the day I was walking around with a huge smile on my face which piqued Janice's interest, so I kept busy moving around the office so that she couldn't get inside my head and start her 101 questions.

By the end of the day, I'd managed to keep away from her and sprang from the office as soon 6 pm hit. I made my way to the grocery to pick up the items that I'd need to make my famous chili, I stopped at the floral section and grabbed some flowers, then headed home to relax. I'm going to need to get a good night's sleep to prepare myself for tomorrow night. Because if everything goes as planned we'll be working off our meals in the bedroom.

Chapter Five

Marissa

"Where are my keys?" I yell upstairs.

Josh comes running down the stairs with his sister following behind him and rounds the corner sliding into the living and throwing himself onto the sofa. He digs in between the cushions and pulls out the keys, Jasmine jumps up and down trying to grab them from his hand as hc holds them in the air.

"Give me, give me. I want to give them to mommy." She pouts, holding her tiny hands in the air as high as she can, trying to grab the keys from him.

"Josh, don't tease your sister," I call out to him as I slip on my heels.

"Here crybaby." He said frowning down at here

"I'm not a baby," she screams at him sticking her tongue out and snatching the keys. "Here you go mommy, have fun on your date." She says with an innocent smile.

The doorbell rings and I open the door to greet my sister then give her a quick hug before dashing out the door and closing it behind me. I get into the car and let out a deep breath then I punch Brendan's address in the GPS and back out of the driveway.

I pull on to his street and continue slowly down the lit-up road looking from house to house noticing that the further

39

down I went the bigger the houses got. Once I reach the end of the street there is a big house that's sitting back into the distance behind a very large gate and for a second, I thought I might've come to the wrong address. I continue up to the gate and come to a stop before rolling my window down and pressing the red button on the speaker box, after a couple of minutes, Brendan's baritone voice comes over the speaker.

"Hey, just a second I'll buzz you in."

"Ok," I quickly reply my voice a little shaky from all the nerves.

A second later a loud buzz sounds, and the gates begin to open. I put the car in drive and continue through the entrance. I pull up and park in front of the house, step out of the car, and smooth out my dress before walking up the stairs to the front door. I'd decided on a short black dress with a pair of stiletto heels for tonight hoping to show off my new and improved body, since the only thing he's really seen me in is sweatshirts, baggy sweatpants, and yoga pants. I still don't understand what it is that this hunk of a man sees in me, but I guess I'll find out soon enough.

The door opens, and he ushers me into the house with a wave of his hand. The way his gaze moved over my body hungrily made me want to leap into his arms and have him take me right here and now.

"Hello Marissa," He said, "My, my, don't you look gorgeous."

He slowly licks his lips then takes my hand into his and kisses the back of it softly. His lips are so big, and his kisses so gentle, it made me want more. I want to feel his lips on my body planting little feather kisses all over me as he slowly

40

makes his way to my chocolate center. Spreading my lips apart with his tongue before kissing my clit.

"Are you ok?" He asks interrupting my thoughts.

"Yes," I reply, and my cheeks flush.

"Please, come in, let me show you around." He said closing the door behind me.

I follow him through the house and as we enter each room, each one was stunning, and the décor is immaculately well put together. It was all too perfect like a woman had decorated the place, and that very thought caused my mind to wander back to his ex-fiancée and whether this was the home he shared with her. But I didn't want to ruin the moment or start bombarding him with questions just yet. When we got to the family room we took a seat on a large burgundy sofa centered in the middle of the room and he shifts his body turning so that he can face me.

"So, what are we having?" I ask trying to get a conversation going so that we could focus on something other than the strong sexual tension between us.

"I don't really cook a lot, but I do make a mean bowl of chili. So, I figure I'll whip that up for you this evening and if you don't like it don't be afraid to tell me, I love getting constructive criticism on my work." He chuckles.

I wanted to jump into the questions that were piercing away at my brain, but now is not the time. Maybe I should wait until we've started eating and then slowly ease them into the conversation, I mean at least then if the conversation goes sour we'll be through with dinner rather then have him kick me out before we've had the chance to eat.

41

The dining room is massive and just as immaculate as the rest of the house. Although the table is quite huge and more so for a dinner party and not a romantic date for two. We ate at the end of the table he sat on the end and I sat next to him on his left side. We quietly dug in for the first 5 minutes and then I opened my big mouth and started hauling out questions.

"This is a beautiful home that you have here, and the décor is breathtaking," I say then pause waiting for him to respond.

"Yeah," he said then paused a moment. "My ex, her name is Nia. She and I shared this home until she left me, and she was the one that decorated the whole place. I would always tell her that she should do it for a living because she's very good at it."

I listened as he continued going into more detail of his failed relationship with Nia and how he keeps telling himself that he's going to have the house redecorated. It's been too much of a reminder and he's ready to walk away from the past that the two of them shared, but he never seems to have the time to get around to it. His eyes were filled with sadness, and I didn't want to press any further, so I changed the subject and allowed him to ask me a few questions.

I told him about my late husband, how much that I missed him, and how his death had a significant impact on myself and our children, but things are a lot easier now. There were plenty of days that I couldn't get out of bed let alone care for the kids or even fix my face to smile. Luckily during those times my mother and my sister were such great helpers. They pulled me out of that rut and I'd went to a few groups for grieving spouses and meet with a therapist twice a week with my children and that helped a great deal as well.

"Well enough about of the sad parts of our lives." He said clearing his throat and taking a sip of wine. "How about we talk about something a little more upbeat, like what are some of your hobbies?"

"Hmm, that's a good question," I say returning a smile. "I love music even though I can't sing a perfect note to save my life I do love listening and playing the piano."

"Oh, very nice. I have a grand piano maybe you can play me a little something after dessert?"

"Sure, I'd love to. I might be a little rusty though it's been awhile since I've played." I said wiggling my fingers then we both laugh.

After we finish with our dessert we take our glasses of wine and head down the hall towards the living room where a piano sat in the middle of the room surrounded by bay windows. Every room in this house is so beautiful, and nothing like what I'm used to. My home is a small and cozy single-family home.

I take a seat on the bench in front of the piano and place my hands on the keys and let out a deep breath. The last time I'd played the piano was the Christmas before my husband passed away and I haven't touched a piano since then.

"Hey, I don't want to bring up sad memories or anything, so you don't have to if you—"

"No, I'm fine." I say cutting him off.

I take another deep breath and close my eyes then slowly begin to move my fingers over the keys. I began playing a melody to a song that I'd written back when my son was born, it was something I would play for him at night to put him to sleep. A wave of emotions washes over me as I remember the very first night that I'd played the song, it was the first night home from the hospital. Josh was crying, and we'd done everything imaginable to soothe him and absolutely nothing was working. So, my husband and I went into the den and I sat down at the piano and began to play the sheet music that I was working on. And as soon as I began to play his sobs turned into magical little ooze that were so beautiful that it touched my heart.

The warm tears ran down my face as I continued to play the piece of music. I moved my hands from the keys and opened my eyes noticing that he'd joined me on the bench. He lifts his hands and wipes away the tears that had fallen from my eyes. His touch ever so gentle as he ran his hand across my cheek then over my bottom lip.

"That was beautiful. You have a very amazing talent there that you're keeping from the world." He says softly.

"Thank you," I reply gazing into his eyes.

His eyes burned with lust and desire as he drew his lower lip between his teeth then leaned in and pressed his lips to mine. I opened my mouth and allowed him access and he deepened the kiss. I melt into his arms as he wraps them around me pulling me closer before moving me onto his lap, so that I was straddling him as the heat between us grew hotter. I unbutton his shirt and pull it open revealing his masculine chest. I could feel the bulge in his pants begging to be set free as I rocked my hips slowly over it.

"Your lips are so soft," he says into my mouth and I kiss him harder. "I want you Marissa, please say that I can have you." He whispers, and I pull away.

I jump from his lap and take a breath as I smooth out my dress. What am I doing? I'm a mother of two children I can't just go around sleeping with the first guy that shows me a little attention. I look up at him and he's staring back at me as sadness and confusion clouds his features.

"I'm sorry I-I have to go," I say stuttering as I scramble around trying to find my things.

"Marissa," He calls out to me. "Did I do something wrong? I'm sorry if I rushed you I didn't mean to." He said, and I could hear the sincerity in his voice, but I had to get out of there.

I rush back to the foyer and grab my purse and my coat that where both hanging by the door and shoot out the front door closing it behind me and rushing down to my car. I get inside and peel out of the driveway towards the gate, once it opened I punched the gas not once hitting the break until both he and his home were in the far distance.

Tears fell into my lap as I drove the rest of the way home.

"I'm so sorry honey," I said aloud repeatedly the entire car ride home. A part of me felt as though I'd almost cheated on my husband, I'd almost giving away a part of me that belonged only to him.

I guess that part of me that believed I was ready to let go and move on was wrong. Because I'm not ready.

Chapter Six

Brendan

It's been a week since I heard from Marissa. I don't know what I did wrong. I saw the look in her eyes she wanted it, she wanted me. So why the hell did she bolt out of the house like it was on fire? I'd taken things slow for that very reason, but I let my guard down and allowed myself to think with my dick instead and I kissed her.

"I should have stopped with the kiss," I said to myself.

I'm sure if I hadn't things would have continued to go smoothly, and we could've continued to have a good time and enjoyed great conversation. But what did I do, I pulled her on top of me and into a deep passionate kiss that I'm sure would've lead to hot and steamy sex on the shag rug in the middle of the room. If we even made it that far.

I've tried calling her several times and I've sent messages apologizing for that night, but she hasn't responded to any of them. Maybe Janice was right maybe I'm not ready for the kind of emotional baggage that she must overcome or maybe it's just too much for someone like me to handle because I have my own.

I let out a loud laugh thinking to myself, "One emotionally broken person trying to help fix another emotionally scarred person." I don't know why I thought that would ever workout. I laugh to myself once again at the thought before gathering myself and falling back into my work.

46

"Hey, are you ok? You've been looked a little down the last couple of days." Janice says poking her head into my office

"Uh, yeah, I'm pretty good," I reply as I put on my best poker face.

"mm-k if you say so. Well, the girls and I are going to head on out if you don't need anything else."

"I'm good, you all enjoy the rest of your evening."

She nods her head and then waves before disappearing from the door. I turn my focus back to my laptop when my phone buzzes I quickly pick it up and flip it over hoping that it was Marissa, but it was my brother Kyle.

"Hey brother, what's going on?" I ask.

"What's going on my main man. I haven't heard from you in awhile where you been hiding or rather I say who have you been hiding in?"

"Hahaha... very funny," I say with a low chuckle. "So, to what do I owe the pleasure of this random call."

"Now why can't I just call to shoot the shit with my younger brother."

"Kyle, you're only older by two minutes," I said emphasizing on the word two.

"Yeah, yeah, yeah I'm still the oldest."

"Whatever," I reply before changing the subject.

My brother and I have always had a very close relationship I mean most would think it was because we're twins but it's a bond that goes much deeper than that. And yes, we have all

47

those telepathic senses that they say twins have. I can sense his pain and him mine which is probably why he's calling.

He carries on making light conversation and telling me all about the new groundbreaking inventions that his company is making and some of the innovative technology that's in the works. My brother owns his own tech company and he's doing quite well for himself and they've just released a new cell phone that's supposed to better than anything out now. My parents thought that we'd both end up in the medical field same as them, but my brother just didn't have the patience, or the mindset of a brain surgeon.

After a full thirty minutes, he finally gets to the real reason as to why he's calling, and I explain my encounter with Marissa and he in turn gave me a few pointers on how I should go about handling things. He's more of the monogamous one and well let's just say I'm more of a free spirit I mean why shouldn't I be. The last woman that I thought was the one walked out on me. Maybe I'm not cut out for the whole relationship thing at least that's what the little voice in the back of my head's been saying, well it was before I meet Marissa now I feel something totally different. I talk to my brother for about another twenty minutes and then we end the call and I get back to work.

"Yo, Brendan you got a sec?" Dawn asks standing in the doorway of my office.

"Yeah, sure come in," I say pointing at the chairs in front of my desk.

Dawn is one of my former colleagues that joined my team when I opened my practice and then there is Jamison who I brought on after he graduated. They've become good friends

48

and everyone in the office has gotten close over the years we've become a family.

After my conversation with Dawn, I decided to head out and grab lunch before my next set of appointments. There's this really good BBQ place that's right down the street from the office and a half rack of ribs was sounding really good and on top of that, I skipped breakfast so I'm starving.

I order a half rack of ribs with a side of mashed potatoes and baked beans from the cute redheaded cashier who cheeks flushed pink as I spoke then took a seat at one of the booths and waited for my food. I pull out my phone and scroll through my emails checking for any new messages as I wait, and I hear a voice that sounds familiar, so I look in that direction. It was Marissa's sister Natalie sitting at a table with two young children and I recognized the little girl that was bouncing in her seat.

Jasmine looked over and notices me looking over at them and her face lit up as she began waving her hand at me in a very quick motion.

"Dr. Hopkins, look aunt Nat it's the doctor that made me all better." She said excited and jumped down out of her seat and started over to me.

"Jazzy where are you going?" Natalie calls out turning in her seat trying to figure out what had gotten Jasmine so excited and she spotted me just as Jasmine reached me and grabbed my hand and began pulling me towards them.

I follow her to the table and greet both Natalie and the little boy at the table who I'd already assumed was her big brother Josh. I shook hands with Natalie and she offered me a seat I

49

knew I wasn't going to be there long, but I figured what the hell why not it's better than waiting alone.

I talked with her and the children until my food was ready and then we said our goodbyes and headed back to the office. Her kids were amazing and very smart and although Josh seemed a little hesitant at first, he started to join in on the conversation. She told me she was babysitting for Marissa until she got off work and that I should stop by the house later and join them for dinner. I said I'd think about it, but I wasn't sure if that was a good idea to show up unannounced especially after what happened that night at my place.

****

I really don't know what I was thinking but somehow, I talked myself into accepting her sister's offer and headed over to Marissa's house after I left work. I'm almost certain that this a bad idea but a part of me wants to see her, talk to her, and be near her. But at the same time, I once again feel like I'm pushing myself on her and not giving her the chance to make a choice in the matter but it's not too late I could always start the car and drive away. It'll be like I was never here, and she never had to know that I actually came by.

I take a deep breath and put my hand on the keys that were still hanging from the ignition. I go to start the car when the front door opens, and Natalie is standing in the doorway staring out looking towards the driveway.

"Brendan is that you?" she asks as she steps out onto the porch.

I hold up my hand to wave at her and a smile appears on her face and I remove my keys opening the door and stepping out. I walk up to the door and she greets me along with a hug before we head inside and Jasmine rushes me again with the same enthusiasm that she'd had earlier at the restaurant.

"Hello again," Jasmine said grinning from ear to ear.

"What's up, Dr. Hopkins," Josh says joining us in the foyer and giving me a fist bump.

"Hey, you all can call me Mr. Brendan you know," I reply, and they nod their head in return. "Is Marissa home?" I ask Natalie and she shakes her head no.

"She's late but she should be here any minute. You can follow me to the dining room though dinner is ready, and it's already set out on the table for us."

Jasmine takes my hand and we all go into the dining room and take our seats. Her home was small, but it was cozy and comfortable you know it had that nice homey feel to it. We fixed our plates and began eating and the kids asked me a quite a few interesting questions some personal and others about being a doctor and Natalie got in a few as well. Then about ten minutes later we hear the front door and Marissa calls out to the kids and her sister as she enters the house.

"Hey, I'm home you guys," She said, "I'm sorry I'm late the restaurant was a madhouse and I had to—" she says then pauses once she entered the dining room and saw me.

She stood frozen in place and all the color drained from her face until Jasmine leaped from her seat and ran over and hugged her. She forced a smile and pulled her into her arms giving her a big bear hug.

"Mommy, mommy look Mr. Brendan came to have dinner with us," Jasmine says in a high-pitched voice.

"I see that was very sweet of him," she says glancing in my direction and then to her sister who was sitting leaned back in her seat with a smirk on her face.

She stands to her feet and walks over to the chair that's next to me and takes a seat grabbing a plate and digging in. We were all about finished so Natalie took the kids into the kitchen so that they could help her clean up. Josh didn't want to, but he agreed anyways because he understood what his aunt meant, and Jasmine was all too thrilled to help with the big girl stuff.

We sat quietly for a few minutes before either one of us said anything and of course it was me who broke the silence.

"I don't know what happen the other night but I'm sorry if I was moving too fast," I say looking over at her and trying to make eye contact, but she doesn't look up.

"It's not you Brendan I—I just got a little scared and I was confused about the way that I was feeling." She pauses and takes a deep breath. "This is all new to me and I don't really know how to feel about it all just yet." She replies in a soft voice.

I look over at her again and then move my chair closer to her and reach over and place my hand under her chin and gently lift her head so that her eyes find mine. I stare into her eyes and it's almost like I can see right through to her soul and like she's looking back into mine.

"It's ok to be afraid Marissa. Honestly, I'm scared shitless to let another woman into my life let alone into my heart again after what happened with my ex." Shit why am I being so open and honest with this woman.

52

She looks back at me tears filling her eyes as she places her hand gently on my cheek. I close my eyes and just take in the moment and the soft touch of her palm against my face.

"I would never hurt you like that Brendan. I ran the other night because I felt as though I was betraying my husband in some way by having another man touch my body so intimately." She says as a stray tear runs down her cheek and I reach over and brush it away.

She moves her hand from my cheek and takes her napkin from its place on the table and wipes away the remaining tears. I was missing her touch, missing the warmth of her hand touching my skin. I wanted her to rest her body onto mine and never leave from it ever again.

Jasmine busts through the kitchen door and yells "Dessert," and we all laugh. She hands us each a slice of Apple pie before returning to her seat.

I helped Marissa wash the dishes after we'd finished dessert then headed into the living room to wait for her while she walked Natalie out and got the kids ready for bed. Hopefully, the rest of the night goes smooth and we end things on a positive note this time without anyone running for the hills.

Chapter Seven

Marissa

I was shocked to walk in and see Brendan sitting at the dining room table having dinner with my family but then again, I wasn't surprised given who my sister is and me explaining to her what had happened the other night. I should've known that she was going to have some kind of plan up her sleeve.

Now that everyone was finished with dinner and had their dessert. I sent Natalie on her way and got the kids into bed so that Brendan and I could have a little adult time.

"Aw, mom, do we have to go to bed? I want to stay up and visit with Mr. Brendan." Jasmine pouted as I tucked her into bed.

"Yes, princess it's time for bed. You can visit with Dr. Hopkins again real soon ok." I reply then lean in and give her a kiss on the forehead.

"Ok, mommy. Oh yeah and he told us to call him Mr. Brendan." She says pulling the cover up over her chest and tucking in her stuffed animal.

"Ok, thanks. I'll try and remember that," I smile back at her and kiss her cheek once more before heading out of the room and closing the door behind me.

I hug my son and tell him goodnight before heading back downstairs. I stop by the kitchen and grab a bottle of wine and two wine glasses then joined him in the living room. I walk in and see him stretched out comfortably on the sofa and his tall frame made my furniture look rather small.

I poured us two glasses of wine then squeezed in beside him handing him a glass before getting comfortable. We clinked our glasses together and then took a sip a together although mine seemed to be a lot longer than his and he watched in amusement.

"Nervous?" He asks with a smile playing on his lips.

"A little," I reply sitting my glass on the table.

Truth is being near him makes me nervous but in a good way. My stomach fills with butterflies and the musky scent of his cologne awakens every part of my body and I just want him to take me. I feel like I'm falling for this man and I've only known him a month now but that didn't stop the desires that filled my body and made me want him more than I've wanted any man.

I want to feel the pulse of his erection as he empties himself inside me as we have a night of rough but passionate sex in front of his fireplace. He clears his throat grabbing my attention as I pull myself away from the steamy thoughts that were still burning in my mind.

His eyebrow was raised and the curious look on his face let me know that he was wondering about what dirty thoughts I was having but not sharing. He chuckles watching me twirl the glass over my lips then reaches over and takes the glass from my hand and sits it on the table.

"Tell me it's ok, say that I can have it," He whispers as he leans in lifting my eyes to meet his.

My breath catches in my throat and his fingers brush across my cheek and down my neck. I shake my head slowly and close my eyes so that I could take in this moment feeling every bit of the intense feelings that came from his lips being pressed against mine. Our tongues danced around, and I melted into his arms pressing his body against mine as he slid down laying me on my back and laying between my legs.

His erection pressed against me rubbing against my sex and I slowly began to move my hips in a slow motion and he smiles into my mouth.

"Wait, Brendan," I say pushing his body away from me a little he pulls back with a look on his face. "Oh gosh, I'm sorry. It's not what your thinking." I continue, and his expression relaxes and his lips twitch into a smile.

"So, you're not going to run again?"

"No, and besides this is my house." I giggle as I push myself up on my elbows. "I was just thinking that this probably isn't the best place to you know. The kids might wake up and come downstairs."

"Oh—right," He said and sits back on the couch adjusting his manhood.

I stare at him while biting my bottom lip. I was beyond turned on and I would give anything to have him fuck me right now, but I don't want to take the chance of one of my kids walking in on the Dr. and I naked on the sofa.

"I should probably get going," he says standing and fixing his clothes.

"Oh, um—ok. Let me walk you out." I reply.

He kisses me on the cheek and opens the door. I stand the doorway watching him as he walks to his car and climbs in. Every ounce of me wanted to run out the door and stop him from leaving but instead, I stood there waving to him as he backed out of the driveway and drove away. I banged my head against the door a couple of times before closing and locking it, and head up to my room.

I stripped down and crawled into bed my head still reeling and my body still craving his touch. I tossed and turned half the night and the other half talking myself out of calling up my sister and having her come over and watch the kids so that I could go and be with the doc.

****

The past couple of weeks have been quite busy, and business has picked up due to the holiday season approaching. People are beginning their Christmas shopping and Thanksgiving was a few days ago so everyone is coming down from their turkey and stuffing binge. But I'm not complaining we were making five times more than our goal intake every single night and probably double on the weekends.

"What's up Mrs. Workaholic?" My good friend Belia says standing in the doorway of my office. "So, there was a pretty hot guy leaving your house and I still don't know who he is, shame on you. I thought you told your best friend everything." She said pouting with her lip sticking out.

I laugh and wave her in. "Hey, I've been so swamped. I'm sorry I haven't had the chance to call and have girl talk." I say as I stand to give her a quick embrace.

"I see business is booming so I guess I can let it slide," she replies giving me a shoulder shrug. "So, you look like you could use a break so that you can tell me all about Mr.—" she pauses waving her hand for me to finish the rest.

"Brendan," I say, and an uncontrollable smile appears on my face. "Dr. Brendan Hopkins to be exact."

"Ah... a doctor. Well look at you, go girl snagging up rich, handsome, and sexy doctors." She said shimmying her shoulders. "So, have we let him spread you wide a give you a full exam yet?" She jokes making her eyebrows dance.

"Oh, gosh, come on Belia," I reply my cheeks flushed.

"What? It's time for you to stop being so stuffy and let a man come and fill the inside—," I hold up my hands in front of me stopping her before she could finish.

I let a scruffy sound and push back my chair turning to place some papers in the file cabinet. She tilts her head to the side and stares at me for a moment then starts to say something else but changes her mind once she sees the look on my face.

"Look, I'm just not ready for that or more like I'm not emotionally ready. My heart hasn't healed from the loss of Chandler yet."

"Chandler is gone, love." She said in a concerned voice. "You're going to have to let go and move on. I mean do you really think he'd want you to be alone for the rest of your life?"

"I suppose not." I sigh.

"uh-uh," she said shaking her finger at me. "So, go on and live a little. I mean you don't have to marry the man just let him get a little taste." She says flicking her tongue.

"You are so nasty."

"I know," she said giggling and standing from her seat. "Alright give me some love, I have to head back to work and you better call me tomorrow young lady."

"Yes, mom will do." I smile and playfully stick out my tongue.

She flips me the finger and then walks out of my office closing the door behind her and leaving me alone with my thoughts once again. It's been a long road and I'm proud of how far I've come after losing the love of my life, but I also understand everyone's concern with me being so closed off. Even though I can see myself falling in love again I'm just not ready right now. I let out the last of the employees and lock the doors before I head back to my office to finish up some paperwork that I hadn't quite gotten to. It took me maybe an hour, but my desk was finally clear of piles of paper and clutter that had accumulated.

I gathered my things and walk to the front of the restaurant and there was a guy standing by the door staring inside and he begins to wave once he sees me. I didn't know the tall husky dark-skinned guy and although he looked friendly, I didn't feel safe unlocking the door for a stranger, so I just spoke through the glass doors.

"Can I help you?" I ask, and he smiles a broad smile back at me.

"Yes, ma'am. Are you Marissa Wilmore?" He asks.

"Uh…yes that's me."

"I'm Ahmad, your driver for the evening."

"But I didn't request a—" and before I could get the rest of the words out my phone chimed.

59

I held my hand up to the man at the door and scrambled for my phone searching through my bag trying to find it. After retrieving it from my bag I clicked on the message, once it opened I saw that it was from Brendan that read.

Brendan: Ahmad (my driver) should arrive in the next five minutes. I can't wait to see you!

I look up at Ahmad then back at the message again, after a couple of seconds I let out a slow breath and unlocked the door stepping outside. I lock up and wiggle the door one last time before turning to face Ahmad.

"Right this way ma'am." He says holding his arm out in front of him.

I smile politely and walk towards the car parked at the curb in front of the restaurant. I pull up my sister's number on my cell and go to press call, but another message comes through right before I press the call button.

Natalie: The kids and I are ok, and I've already made dinner. Enjoy your night with the doc!

I shake my head and relax back in my seat watching as the buildings blurred by until we eventually slow down and came to a stop in front of a Boutique shop. The mannequins in the window were dressed in long and flowing gowns that were so beautiful and elegant. Ahmad stepped out of the SUV and came around to open my door extending his hand and helping me out.

"They're waiting for you inside," Ahmad said holding his hand out towards the door.

"Thank you," I say offering him a warm smile.

I walk into the Boutique and a slender young woman with braid flowing down to her waist greeted me as soon as I entered.

"Hello, you must be Marissa. We've been waiting for you, come right this way." She says with a wide smile.

We go to the back and walk through a curtain that leads to a small dressing room in the back. A dress was draped out over the chaise and a pair of red bottom heels were placed beside it. The dress was so stunning the sequence and the beading was perfectly placed.

"Is this for me?" I ask my eyes bulging out of my head.

"Yes, ma'am. I'll step out and let you get dressed and when you're ready we will head over to hair and make-up." She said then disappeared through the curtains.

I nod my reply because my mind wouldn't form the words. I've never had anyone do anything like this for me and not that my husband wasn't romantic, but he'd never done anything like this. I guess there are some excellent perks of being a doctor and having a huge cash flow also she knew him by name, so he must come here a lot or perhaps he sends other ladies here that he's dating.

Hmm... Nope, stop it, Marissa, don't go getting in your head or thinking too much. Maybe he'd called the store or dropped by to set all of this up is all and if, so he has excellent taste. I'll make a mental note to ask him about it later tonight.

I slip into the dress and man did it hug to my every curve tight like a glove. I was a little skeptical at first when I looked at myself in the mirror because I've never really been comfortable showing off my body in such a way. I was more accustom to dresses that were a bit freer flowing and I've never had the body of a supermodel, so I'll say that I'm insecure when it comes to my curves.

"You look absolutely perfect in that dress," she says stepping back into the room.

"Thank you. But it seems so…tight," I reply looking in the mirror sucking in a breath.

"Nonsense you look gorgeous and the dress is amazing."

She winks then motions for me to follow her and I do so. We walk down a hall that leads into a completely different space. One side had a salon and the other a make-up bar. I was already wearing make-up, so she just touched it up and after the stylist was finished pulling my curls into a sleek bun that rested at the nape of my neck, I was out the door and on my way to my next destination.

We arrived at an event hall and Ahmad pulled up to the curb and helped me out of the SUV. He walked me to the door where I was greeted by a very attractive older guy that took my arm and lead me inside. I looked back at Ahmad and smiled before waving goodbye and he waved in return and smiled before exiting the building.

My heart felt like it was going to burst through my chest as we walked towards a set of huge wooden doors. I could hear music playing so I knew that we were about to enter some sort of gathering but I didn't know what kind. The doors opened and two men in tuxedos ushered us in, my eyes quickly searched the room in search of Brendan and I spot him standing with a group of men laughing.

I nod to the gentleman that escorted me inside and begin to make my way over to Brendan. As I stroll through the crowd our eyes meet and his gaze falls from my face down to the skin-tight dress and a sexy smirk plays on his lips.

He turns and says something to the group of men I guess excusing himself then leaves the group and walks over to me. He takes my hand and leads me out of the crowded room and down a long hall to a room at the end. Once we were inside he closed the door behind us locking it.

"Brendan what are—" I began but his mouth suddenly crashes into mine kissing me feverishly as he pins my body to the wall.

"Pull up your dress," he says into my mouth.

I do as I'm told, and he wraps his arms around my waist lifting me off the ground. I put my legs around his waist and my arms around his neck, gazing into his eyes. They were filled with lust send a tingling feeling all over me. My pussy ached for his touch. I could feel the overwhelming need for pleasure between the two of us I'd felt it the very first time we'd spoken that day at the gym.

He continued to kiss me, and I lose all control deepening the kiss. My panties were soaked, and I needed to feel him inside of me. My body was screaming for to be touched and driven to an orgasmic release. I mean this can't be healthy, all this sexual tension and torture that were putting ourselves through.

"I want you, I want you now, Brendan," I said pleading with him and he stops abruptly placing me back on the ground and taking a step back. "What—what's wrong? Brendan, I'm

63

ready, I want you." I say confused as to why he'd stopped so suddenly.

"No," he says shaking his head.

"No. Why no?" I say still struggling to even my breaths. "I'm telling you that you can have me, I'm offering myself to you and now you're saying no."

"I'm sorry, Marissa." He said, "Let's go back to the party, ok. I'll give you a second to straighten yourself up."

He walks out the room and stands in the hall waiting for me to compose myself so that we can head back to the party. I don't understand what just happened I know that he wants me so why is he holding back. Maybe I messed up, maybe I waited too long and now he doesn't want me anymore.

I blink back the tears that threatened to escape my eyes and take a deep breath exhaling slowing before walking over to the door. I put on a fake smile and walked out, he was pacing back and forth and froze in place once the door was opened.

"Shall we," He says after a second holding out his hand for mine.

I nod and take his hand then he leads me back down the hall to the party room where everyone was still laughing, dancing, and having a good time. When we walked in it seemed like every eye in the room was on us or probably on me. The men were all dressed in tuxedos and the women were dressed in what looked to be very expensive ball gowns. We walked around the room and he introduced me to a lot of big names in the medical world as well as two of the doctors from his practice.

We finally made our way over to a table in the corner of the room and sat down. I was all too eager to get comfortable in a seat because these heels were turning out to not be my friend. My feet were killing me, I don't know how these women do it walk around in stiletto heels all night.

"You look gorgeous," Brendan says breaking me away from my thoughts.

"Thanks," I say smiling up at him. "You have excellent taste and a very good eye might I add. How'd you know my size?" I asked curious to know.

"Your sister." He said and chuckled.

"Ah... I see." I respond with an eye roll. "Well, this was sweet of you and thanks for making me feel like a princess for a night."

"You mean a queen," he corrects me. "I do believe princess is already taken by a lovely little lady named Jasmine." He says winking at me.

I snap my finger and say. "You know what your right."

We both laugh and just like that the night was restored back to the way it was in the beginning. The charity event began, and we sat quietly enjoying the rest of the evening together. At the end of the night, Brendan is presented with a Nobel prize and he looked so handsome as he walked on stage to accept his award.

After we said our goodbyes we headed out to the SUV where Ahmad was waiting for us and climbed inside. The ride was quiet and when we reached my house he walked me to the door and kissed me goodnight, then returned to the SUV and they drove away. I was every bit of confused as any human could possibly be and horny as hell. I mean why would he take me into that room and get us both all hot and bothered only to push me away.

He was hiding something. Then it dawned on me perhaps I wasn't the only one still holding on to a past love. Maybe he's still in love with his ex-fiancée and hasn't moved past the hurt.

Chapter Eight

Brendan

She was so responsive, so wet, and ready. But I couldn't do it. Even though she had given me permission to take her and do whatever it was that I wanted to her, I just couldn't.

I've asked myself why every day since the award ceremony, but I just can't seem to wrap my mind around it. I'm confused and sexually frustrated. My heart still belongs to Nia but my body—my body wants Marissa. What the hell is happening to me, I've seen Nia and I've met her husband. She's also made it very clear that she's moved past me. She'd moved on and she'd taken my heart with her but the day that she was in my office she'd given it back to me ripped to shreds.

I could tell the words she spoke were sincere and deep down inside I knew that it was the closure I needed, so why am I still moping around like an injured animal? I have a gorgeous, loving, and caring woman that wants me, but I can't seem to let go and mend my broken heart so that I can open myself up to her.

A knock on my office door got my attention and I look up to find Jamison in the doorway.

"Hey, what's up?" I say waving him inside.

"Nothing much, I just have a quick question." He said entering my office and stopping a few steps away from my desk. "I was wondering if you could cover for me on

Thursday. It's my daughter's birthday and I want to try and leave early so that the two of us can hang out."

"Of course, that shouldn't be a problem. Just let Janice know so that she can make the changes to our schedules before you leave." I reply.

"Thanks, Brendan I really appreciate it." He said with a sad expression on his face.

His divorce was really taking a toll on him and not being able to see his daughter as much, is taking an even bigger one. This was his second marriage and it was ending after twelve years, gosh twelve years is a long time, so I can only imagine how he's feeling. He didn't have kids with his first wife and they'd married young not really knowing what they were getting into. So, when things fell apart they mutually agreed to separate but this time it wasn't mutual, and he adores his baby girl so being away from her must be killing him on the inside.

As I thought about Jamison's situation, Marissa and her two children crossed my mind. The thought of how painful it would be to lose them once I let them into my life and into my heart. Could I bare that kind of heartbreak? Would she still allow me to come around if we were no longer together?

Princess Jasmine has already begun to pull at my heartstrings and that was only after a couple weeks. The way that she's taken a liking to me and the sweet sound of her adorable voice calling out to me and the cute little way that she messes up my name when she says it has already gotten to me.

"I can't do this," I say rubbing my hands over my face. I grab my notepad and the file for my last patient for the evening and head down to the exam room.

Once I left the office I stopped by the gym for a quick workout before heading home. I got a good two hours of intense cardio in and hit the punching bag a little before I called it a night and headed home. I was feeling good and sort of relaxed now that I'd blown off a little steam because the heavens know that this sexual tension between Marissa and I is driving me insane.

I pull through the gate and park in front of the door instead of in the garage. I unlock the door and walk into the house dropping my gym bag and briefcase before hanging my coat.

I turn on the shower and get undressed. I normally would have showered before leaving the gym but the airs a bit chilly tonight as the weather is changing. I let the hot water run over my body massaging and relaxing my muscles and I think to myself damn I'm glad I let Nia talk me into having these shower jets installed.

Oh no, why did I let her name creep up in my mind? Flashes of her full breast and luscious chocolate nipples appear vividly behind my closed eyes, and me on my knees as she rests her back against the shower wall, her leg over my shoulder as I lick her sweet pink center. She loved it when I fucked her in the shower and remembering her bent over and her ass clapping as I took her from behind filling her deep with every inch of me still made my dick hard.

My eyes shot open when I heard the sound of my cell ringing, so I shook the thought from my mind and shut off the shower, open the door, and stepped out grabbing one of the towels and wrapping it around me.

I pick up my phone and see a message from Janice confirming the times for the two patients of Jamison's that were added to my list of appoints this coming Thursday. I throw my phone on to the bed and walk back into the bathroom walking over to the mirror and wiping away the fog and staring at myself through the glass disappointment lingering as my hopes of a call from Marissa faded.

"Get your shit together Brendan," I say to myself exhaling a long breath before picking up my toothbrush and brushing my teeth.

I go into the closet and grab a pair of pj bottoms and pull them on before heading back downstairs to the bar and pulling myself a glass of bourbon. After making myself some soup I take it to my room and eat up then down another glass of bourbon while I watch old Kung Fu movies.

The next day at the office everything went smooth, all my patients were on time, and there were no cancelations which didn't happen too often. By the end of the day I was beat and starving I never got around to grabbing lunch, but luckily one of the young ladies that's interning here rounded up everyone's order and made a food run.

"Here you go sir, one chicken teriyaki sub and a Pepsi." She says her face lit up as she placed the food on my desk.

"Thanks," I replied returning the smile.

She bounces out the door cheerfully her ponytail swinging from left to right as she walked away. The sub was delicious and just what I needed to get me through the rest of the day which was going to be coming to an end in a few hours.

"Hey, you got a sec?" Dawn said poking her head around the corner like she usually does at the end of the day.

"Sure," I wave her in and she enters taking a seat in front of my desk pulling the chair closer and crossing her arms on top.

I figured she'd just come to talk about one of her patients or ask me a medical question. But from the look on her face and her whole demeanor, I quickly got the vibe that this was going to be something entirely different.

"I need to ask you a kind of personal question, is that ok?" She said squeezing her eyes together but peeking out of one.

"Uh-yeah go ahead ask away," I say.

"Ok," she said excitedly. "There is a man that I'm interested in but he's kind of going through something at the moment." She says talking with her hands. "And I don't want to come off as being pushy, so I just wanted to get a guy's take on how I should go about approaching him."

I stare at her with a blank expression not sure if I should ask her who this mystery guy is even though I think I have a pretty good clue of who she's referring to. And knowing how hard it is to break down the walls of a man who's had his heartbroken takes time and a lot of patience.

"And might I ask who this guy is and what exactly is his situation?" I ask, with a raised eyebrow.

"Well," she paused glancing at the ceiling. "Let's just say that he's recently ended a long-term relationship, but the chemistry between us is unmatched. And I'm kind of already starting to develop feelings for him."

I take a deep breath and lean on to my desk placing my hands together. "All I can tell you to do is take it slow. He's going to need time to heal and if you two have hit off the way you

71

say then just go with the flow and allow him to fall back when he needs to."

She takes a deep breath and blows it out quickly after hearing me out and even though I'm sure my words weren't the ones she wanted to hear it was my honest opinion on the situation. Especially being that I'm dealing with the same kind of situation currently made me realize that I needed to take my own advice and give Marissa a call tonight and see if she wants to meet up.

After everyone left the office I locked up and stayed a little later to catch up on some paperwork and emails that I didn't have the chance to get this afternoon. About thirty minutes later I set my pen down on my desk and relax in my chair stretching out a bit when I hear a knock on the glass at the front of the office. I get up from my chair and walk out into the hall and glance through the window of the receptions desk and I see Marissa standing at the door.

She looked cold, so I rushed to the door and unlocked it letting her in.

"Hey," she said as I opened the door. She stood smiling up at me her cheeks and nose a light shade of red.

"What are you doing here?" I asked surprised that she'd come all the way into town.

"I wanted to see, and I wasn't sure what time you got home, so I called earlier, and your assistant told me you'd be here late."

Janice, why hadn't she told me that Marissa had called me today. Perhaps it was because we were really busy today but either way, I would ask her about it Monday morning when she returned to work.

"Well come in you must be freezing," I step to the side so that she could come in then closed the door and locked it. "Follow me we have some hot cocoa in the back I'll make you a cup," I say taking her hand.

Her hands were so cold I leaned over and wrapped my hands around hers blowing inside my hands trying to warm them up. Her mouth curved into a smile as she gazed into my eyes and for a moment I was lost in them it was like she had me mesmerized. When she moved her hands from mine I blinked quickly a couple of times and then got up to make her a cup of cocoa.

I handed her the cup and she took it eagerly blowing into it before taking a sip. I watched as her face relaxed and she closed her eyes savoring the chocolatey goodness. She followed me back to my office and took a seat in front of my desk and I took a seat behind my desk powering down my laptop and closing it.

"I'm happy that you dropped by to surprise me." I say, "This was meant to be a surprise, right? Or was there another reason you came by?" I was curious as to why the unexpected visit, especially after the other night.

"Well…the answer is actually yes to both questions."

"Oh, really," I reply my interest now piqued.

"Mm-hmm…" she says placing her cup on the desk and rising from her seat and walking around the desk stopping directly in front of me.

She slowly unbuttons the long coat that she's wearing that covered her entire body then slowly unzipped it and let it fall off her shoulders and on to the floor. My mouth dropped, and my dick twitched in my pants as I looked her up and down she was wearing a red bra with matching lace panties.

"You really shouldn't come out the house like that you could catch a cold," I say my tone playful.

"Oh, don't you worry," she replies straddling me, pressing her breast against my chest as she leaned in and whispered, "I know a very handsome doctor that'll take good care of me if that happens." She said kissing my earlobe then trailing soft kisses down my neck and I lean my head back on to the chair giving her full access.

She kissed my chest after undoing each button on my shirt until it was completely undone running both of her hands over my chest until she reached the bulge in my pant. She looked into my eyes as she unfastened my belt and then my pants unleashing my massive erection. With a smile on her face, she took me into her hand and stroked my dick taking her time admiring and appreciating the size and length.

I liked this side of her the side that was untamed and not afraid to take charge. I knew she had it in her, but she just needed a little help bringing it out of her and I'm sure my rejection the other night had a lot to do with her surprise visit.

I cup her beast in my hand and raise it to my mouth teasing her nipple with my tongue before gently pulling it between my teeth. She let out a soft moan that made me all the more eager to dive deep inside of her, but I needed to be patient I wanted to take my time getting to know her body. I push my

74

laptop to the side and push the rest of the things onto the floor before laying her on top of my desk.

I put her legs on each side of my shoulders and pull her to the edge of the desk sliding my hands under her ass and tilting it up. Her pussy is beautifully groomed, and the aroma is mouthwatering I was desperate to taste her. I kissed her lips then used my tongue to spread them lightly blowing on her clit before letting my tongue circle her sweet spot, teasing, and sucking it each time.

"Relax," I whisper feeling her legs getting tense.

I rub my hands down her inner thighs and then slide one finger inside of her and she gasps arching her back. She's so tight and so ready for me her juices ran down my finger as I slowly moved them in and out of her and after a few seconds her body relaxed, and she began to rock her hips matching my movement. I add another finger then lean forward and get back to stimulating her clit with my mouth, I feel her walls tightening around my fingers, so I move in and out of her faster.

"Brendan," she moans as she rocks against my fingers thrusting her pelvis until she goes over the edge reaching her full orgasm. Her legs were trembling as I removed them from my shoulders allowing her to place her feet on the desk.

Hearing her moan my name made my dick harder. I admired her body as she laid naked across my desk her body is perfect she had curves in all the right places and her ass is so nice and round. I couldn't help myself I wanted to take her from behind I pulled her up from the desk and flipped her over onto her stomach.

Her breath hitched, and she turned pushing her hair out of her face so that she could look back at me. I took my dick in my hand and rubbed it between her lips before slowly sliding inside of her taking my time so that she could adjust to my size.

"Damn," is all that I could manage once I was inside of her.

Chapter Nine

Marissa

"Brendan, please," I begged needing more of him.

He was moving so painfully slow and I wanted more, I wanted all of him inside of me, fucking me hard until my pussy was numb from beating. His tongue felt incredible and damn if he didn't know all the right spots to hit sending my pussy into a multi-orgasmic frenzy.

My body was doing things that I never knew it was capable of I've had at least 3 orgasms and I didn't even know that was possible. He slammed into me his thrusting getting faster as he pumped harder, pushing deeper inside of me. I felt his dick spasm and his body tenses as he climaxed spilling his seeds deep inside of me as he let out a low growl.

"Ah fuck," He said leaning forward and placing his hands on the desk.

He kissed the back of my neck and the back of my head before getting up and pulling himself out of me slowly. He left the room to go and get a couple of towels from the supply room then wets them and hands me one to clean myself off. I walk over to the pile on the floor where I left my coat and shoes and quickly remembered that I'd come in just a coat.

"Umm," I said getting his attention. "Can you do me a favor?"

"Yeah sure."

"I kind of need my bag and it's in the trunk of my car," I say, and he smiles back at with that smile that makes my heart stop.

"Oh, ok, where are your keys?"

I go over and pick up my coat and grab my keys out of the pocket and toss them to him. He reaches out and catches them with ease then winks at me before walking out the office and a couple of seconds later I hear the bell on the door jingled.

I slip on my panties and my bra and then take a seat on the cream-colored couch in the corner of his office. A couple of seconds later he appeared with my bag and I quickly dressed then took my seat back on the couch where I sat quietly waiting for him to say something, anything, the silence in the room was deafening.

I needed to know what he was thinking, what he was feeling. We'd just had amazing mind-blowing sex and he was just sitting there not saying a word. He didn't even bother to come and sit next to me or hold me in his arms afterward gosh not even a kiss. Maybe this was a mistake I mean I did just throw myself at him and there is no man in the world that's going to turn down sex. "I really need to get the hell out of here!" I think to myself. The air in the room thickens and my chest tightens, and it feels like I can't breathe.

"So, I guess I should get going." I say standing and grabbing my bag and sliding it on to my shoulder.

I get my coat and head for the door glancing back at him one last time before walking out of his office. Why isn't he

78

stopping me I think as I continue towards the front door as tears filled my eyes and I blink them away quickly.

"Marissa, wait!" He called out to me and stopped right where I was.

I feel his movements as he walks over to me placing his arms around me, pushing my hair back behind my shoulder, then kissing my cheek. I relaxed in his arms and closed my eyes breathing in the scent of his aftershave and leaning my head against him.

"Don't leave," he whispers in my ear.

"I was hoping you would say that," I reply dropping my bag to the floor and turning to face him.

He reached under my chin and lifted my face and his lips find mine as he kisses me softly.

He gathers his things and we walk out to the parking lot together and get in our separate cars. I follow him back to his place and as soon as we walk through the door it was on once he locked the door our bodies collided, and our clothes were flying left and right as we quickly pulled them off. I'm not sure of when we'd gotten to the room, but we eventually made it there but not to the bed we made love right there on the floor in front of the bed.

"What are you thinking?" He asks, stroking my hair while I lay on his chest.

"You really want to know?" I say pulling the cover over my breast and sitting up so that I could look at him.

"Yes."

"It may seem weird because we just finished having sex, but I was actually thinking about my kids," I say, and he looks at me with a quizzical expression on his face, so I continue. "What I mean is I was thinking of how I should explain what this is," I say moving my hands back and forth between us.

"Oh," He responds his expression changing to a wary one. "Well, what exactly do you think this is? Don't we have to sort of figure that out ourselves before we can actually add a title to it for them."

"Right," I respond quickly.

He was right we were going to have to figure out what we were doing before bringing the kids in on this. Ugh, why did I have to open my big mouth and tell him what I was really thinking I should've just made something up or just said nothing. I change the subject to a much lighter conversation and we spend the rest of the night talking and enjoying each other's company.

The next morning, I awake to an empty spot next to me and a note on his pillow that read.

Didn't want to wake you,

you looked so peaceful.

I'll be back asap just

making a quick coffee run.

I smile and set the note on the bedside table. I go into the bathroom that was huge pretty much the same size as my master bedroom and bathroom combined. I searched for a towel and a washcloth so that I could take a quick shower and get dressed before he returned. As I was looking I found a towel and washcloth neatly folded on a stool beside the bathtub that was filled bubbles that smelled of lavender and vanilla. I dip my hand into the water and it was warm all I had to do was climb inside and relax.

He'd drawn me a bath before going out to grab coffee and breakfast for us gosh could this man be more perfect. I ease into the water flinching a little as the warm water brushes my sex, I pause and take in a deep breath then I slid into the water once again.

Sex with Chandler was always slow and passionate, and he took his time when we made love. Sex with Brendan is something totally different he's rough and aggressive even the way that he touches me, pulling my hair, and gripping my thighs as he pushes deep inside me is a whole new experience for me. The pain that I feel is just a reminder of him being there and leaving my mind to remember each and every moment of the night even now just thinking about it is arousing.

Once he returned we ate our breakfast and talked about how our week had gone. Before I left we made plans to get together tomorrow night, he wanted to take me and the kids out to dinner so that he could spend some time with all of us together. And I agreed besides I think it's sweet that he wants to include my children in our night out or that he wanted to get to know them at all and that alone was the reason that I'm falling for him even more.

For most men, sex is enough and including the kids in the relationship causes things to get complicated or, so they say. But so far everything about Dr. Brendan Hopkins is different but we'll see how long he sticks around once he gets a glimpse of how life really is with two kids.

Chapter Ten

Marissa

I decided to have a girl's day with my sister and my two besties so that we could all catch up with each other and what was better than sipping wine and getting Mani & Pedi's at the spa. And we deserved it being the boss moms that we are called for a little R&R every now and again and on top of that, we haven't seen much of each other lately because of our busy schedules and of course our kids.

"So, tell me how things are going with the oh so hot and hunky doctor?" Belia asks her face bubbly and her eyes filled with curiosity.

"Oh, yes, sis please tell us about your romp in the sheets with the doc." Natalie insisted as Trista shook her head in agreeance.

I sit quietly not saying a word sipping my wine as they watch me with piercing eyes, but I just smiled and closed my eyes laying my head back on the cushioned headrest.

"Oh, no she didn't," Belia said leaning forward in her seat. "I know you better spill it miss missy." She demanded snapping her fingers at me.

"Alright, alright. Geez, why are you all so interested in my sex life anyway." I joke.

I tell them about the other night when I surprised him at his office in nothing, but my red lace bra and panties set. I didn't

83

go into too much detail because a woman should never tell all the juiciness of her man's thrust and stroke but what little info they got left them speechless.

By the time we'd finished, our Pedi's the spotlight was shifted from me and on to Trista and her boo. She'd been dating her boo for a year and a half and they'd never had sex I mean we were starting to think that he was gay for a moment there. Don't get me wrong I'm all for doing things the right way and saving yourself for marriage but neither of them is virgins and he never gave her a reason as to why.

"If I were you—," Belia began but Trista cut her off.

"Well, you're not so let's not go there, please." Trista snaps at her.

We all turn and look over at Trista with a surprised look on our faces. She was always the quiet one and she never got snappy or even said anything to defend herself, but today she was full of comebacks and I liked it. Everyone remained silent while the techs finished up our pedicures and we had lunch and then we said our goodbye's then we went our separate ways.

I drove to my parents and picked up the kids so that I could head home and get dinner started. But when I call my mom to tell her that I was on the way I could hear Jasmine in the background screaming that she wanted to stay with her papaw and Josh wasn't ready to leave his friends. So, I decided to let them stay the night since my parents were already cool with it.

I headed home alone prepared to order take out and sit in my jammies watching movies and eating the chubby fudge ice cream right out of the container. I didn't like being alone, but at the same time, I loved getting a break from the kids every now and again just so that I could have a little peace and quiet for at least one night. My phone rings and I press the button on the wheel answering it.

"Hey, you," I say with a huge smile on my face.

"Hello gorgeous," He replied, "So what time should I pick up the kids for our date."

I pause for a second realizing that I'd forgotten about our date with the kids for tonight and let out a long sigh.

"Oh, no. I'm sorry, Brendan, I forgot about our date with the kids. They wanted to spend the night with my parents and Jasmine was getting fussy, so I told them that they could say."

He chuckled, "Hey, it's ok. We can always get together another time."

"That sounds great."

"So," He said pausing for a second, "What are you getting into tonight now that you're kid free."

I let a few seconds past before I answered I mean I didn't really think that telling him about my plan to have takeout and then devour a whole pint of chubby fudge while binge-watching one of those reality TV shows that I almost never have time to watch was a good idea. It actually would have sounded lame, so I responded with something simple.

"I think I'm going to grab something to eat and then head home and have a peaceful night in."

"Oh. Ok. Well, that sounds very boring." He laughs, "maybe I should come over and keep you company tonight."

He'd read my mind because that was exactly what I was thinking so I tell him to meet me at my place in 15 minutes I needed to go to the grocery and grab a few things for dinner before I headed home. I hadn't really planned on cooking but the least I could do is feed the man before he has my toes touching the headboard.

I pull into the parking lot and rush in the store and grab a pack of chicken breast, broccoli, and cheese so that I can make stuffed chicken. I really don't know what type of foods that he enjoys so I went for the most simplest thing and if he doesn't like the broccoli I can always remove it. I chat with the checkout girl as she scans my items then I rush out to the car and hop inside quickly pulling out of my spot and shooting east towards my house. I pull into the garage and I was happy that I'd made it home before he arrived I hurried and grabbed my purse and the bags and dashed into the house throwing the chicken and broccoli in the fridge and the other things on the counter so that I could go and freshen up.

I changed out of my jeans into a pair of yoga pants and an oversized sweatshirt that was my favorite. I pull my long tresses into a loose bun on top of my head and apply a little lip gloss to my lips and blow out a deep breath before heading back downstairs. The doorbell rings just as my feet touch the last step and I quickly jog over to the door to open it and as soon as I opened the door it was like all the air had left my lungs as I looked at him in my doorway. He was breathtaking in his jeans and a red polo shirt that hugged his body nicely showing off his toned chest and arms my ovaries were doing flips as the sweet spot between my legs smiled with excitement.

"Is it ok if I come in?" He asks breaking my concentration.

86

"Yes, of course," I giggle stepping aside, "I'm sorry, come inside."

I shut the door behind him then turn on my heels and head towards the kitchen to get started on our meal. He follows me into the kitchen and takes a seat in the chair in front of the Island as I gather all the ingredients and place them on the counter near the stove. I pull out the cutting board and place it on the counter and then begin prepping the chicken so that I could stuff it. I could feel his eyes watching me as I moved around the kitchen and I would catch a glimpse of the smile on his face out the side of my eye every time I turned to the stove.

"I can help if you'd like." He said getting up from his seat and joining me near the stove placing his hand on my lower back.

My breath hitched, and I closed my eyes as his hands slide around my waist and he pulled me back into his chest kissing my neck and then my ear. I turned in his arms and put my arms loosely around his neck and gazed into his eyes for a second before I spoke.

"You know if you keep touching me like that then I won't be able to finish up our dinner," I say giving him a soft smile.

He dips down a little and pulls his arms around me tighter, pulling me into him more before lifting me off my feet causing me to giggle. "Maybe I'm in the mood for something sweet. Can I have a taste of your sweet pink spot, Marissa." He says with a smirk on his face.

I bit my bottom lip as I stare back into his hazel eyes and they pull me in even deeper. I wrap my legs around him and press my lips to his and our tongues begin to move feverishly as we kiss passionately. He breaks away from the kiss and turns off the oven and carries me out of the kitchen and up the stairs to my bedroom. He lays me on the bed and pulls off my yoga pants, and his lips part into a small smile when he noticed that I wasn't wearing any panties. He threw my pants to the side then pulled his shirt over his head and tossed it to the side along with them before sliding in between my legs.

He kissed the inside of my thighs before letting his tongue slide between my swollen lips brushing over my clit making my legs tremble. I arched my back and grabbed onto the sheets as he took me into his mouth sucking and licking my clit while his fingers filled me, pressed in and out, curing the ache and need. My hips rocked to the rhythm of his thrust as the pleasure continues to build inside of me and when I was right at the edge, my hips thrust into him faster until my orgasm ripped through me and my juices gushed all over him.

He kissed my pussy one last time before standing and removing his jeans and then his boxers letting his erection spring free and a smile spread across my face and he chuckled. I'd longed to fill his long thick shaft pumping inside of me ever since the night we'd had sex in his office a few weeks ago. He leaned down on the bed and pulled my legs together, flipping me over on to my belly, and letting his tongue run up my spine and back down again. I gasped and then let out a soft moan as he slid his fingers between my thighs and slide two of them inside of me and the sound that my juices were making as he pushed in and out turned me on even more.

"Are you ready for me baby," he whispered as he kissed my back.

"Yes…" I moaned.

He removed his fingers and lifted my ass just a little before taking his dick in his hand and rubbing between my lips, parting them, and easing inside of me slowly.

"Omgosh," I whispered.

He moved in and out of me slowly for a minute and then began to pick up the pace. He felt so good inside of me and my pussy it fit around his dick like a glove squeezing him tighter and tighter each time that I reached an orgasm and after my third orgasm, I felt his dick spasm as he let out a groan deep in his throat. He thrust harder and deeper inside of me as we both rode out or orgasm and then he pulled out and fell onto the bed beside me. We both lie on the bed panting trying to catch our breaths for several minutes before he rolled over and put his arm around me pulling me closer to him.

He kisses the back of my neck and smiles pulling his arm tighter around me and I close my eyes and enjoying this moment. It's been so long since I've had a man put his arms around me and cuddle up beside me so that we could spoon after having hot and steamy sex.

"So, how about that meal you promised me." He jokes and we both laugh.

We get up and get dressed or particularly, I slip on his polo shirt and he grabbed his jeans sliding them on before we head down to the kitchen. He cuts the broccoli and I continue to prep the chicken before stuffing it with the ingredients which I showed him how to do because he was so eager to help. Once the chicken was inside the oven we sat at the island and had a glass of wine until it was finished then headed into the dining room to eat.

"Now isn't this better than a quiet night alone?" He asks placing a fork full of broccoli into his mouth.

"Mm… I don't know, I mean chilling on the sofa in my pjs with a pint of chubby fudge just might be a little more enticing." I teased, winking at him.

"Oh really." He raises his brow. "So, you're telling me chubby fudge is better than a toe curling orgasm, actually it was three toe-curling orgasms if I'm not mistaking."

I gasp and stare over at him with a surprised look on my face and chuckles while stuffing his mouth with last of the chicken, cheese, and broccoli on his plate. I couldn't believe that he'd said that then again no I wasn't seeing as to how he hasn't been afraid to speak his mind from the moment I meet him.

"Well, maybe we should go back up to the bedroom and see if you can beat your previous record," I say leaning in closer to him.

"That sounds like a challenge," He said, "I'm not sure that you'll be able to handle it I mean you were about to tap out after just three a few moments ago."

I laugh. "I guess we will just have to see," I say softly walking over and gently kissing his lips and before I knew it he had scooped me up and thrown me over his shoulder and smacking me on the ass and heading back to the room.

****

I roll over and open my eyes as the sunshine's bright throughout my entire room and close my eyes and open then opening them again blinking a few times until they'd adjusted. I look over to my left to see him sleeping on his side with his back turned to me and I smile to myself happy that he hadn't gotten up and snuck out in the middle of the night. I get up and go into the bathroom and use the restroom then wash my hands and brushed my teeth noticing that my hair was all over the place as I looked in the mirror, so I pulled the hair tie from my head and let my hair fall down over my shoulders.

I used my hands to comb through it some and then pushed it back from my face taking one last look in the mirror before heading out of the bathroom.

"Good morning gorgeous," He said with a sexy grin on his face.

"Good morning," I reply my cheeks heating up as I smile back at him.

He looked so at home and comfortable sitting in my bed looking so yummy with his dreads pulled to the top of his head as he sat with his back against the headboard and his cell in his hand.

"Are you hungry? I can go and make us some breakfast if you are."

"No, I'm fine. How about you come back to bed."

"My, someone has a very energized libido," I joked walking back over to his side of the bed and climbing on top of him.

"I can't resist you when you're walking around with my shirt on." He said leaning forward, kissing me, and letting his hands slide down to my ass and I gently bite his bottom lip and I feel him getting excited.

He slips his hand under his shirt and cups my breast in his hand, gently massaging it as I lean my head back slightly and close my eyes. He pushes my hair back and kisses my neck, my collarbone, and just as he began to lift my shirt so that he could have access to what was underneath I hear a loud gasp come from the doorway and I turned to see my mom standing there.

"Oh, my word." She said quickly covering her eyes with her hands.

"Omgosh. Mom. What are you doing here?" I say jumping from Brendan's lap and covering myself with the sheet.

"I'm sorry, sweetheart. Your father took the kids to the movies, so I thought I'd come over and see if you wanted to go and get breakfast. But I see you've already had your meal this morning."

"Oh, gosh, mom please can you go and wait for me downstairs."

"Okay, I'm going." She says waving her hand in the air but not before winking in Brendan's direction.

I was so embarrassed, I couldn't even look over at him. I just wanted to crawl under the covers and into the fetal position and not come out for the rest of the day. When I removed my hands from my face he was smiling over at me and I couldn't help but smile back and we both burst into laughter. I couldn't believe my mom had just walked in on me about to have sex with Brendan, but I guess I was glad that it was her and not one of the kids or my sister now that I think of it I really need to set some rules.

I change into a pair of shorts and a t-shirt and go downstairs to talk to my mom. She was seated at the island in the kitchen with a glass of orange juice and I walk over to the cabinet and grab me a glass and pour myself some before joining her.

"Geez mom do you ever knock?" I roll my eyes and let out a deep breath.

"I said I was sorry, sweetheart. I didn't no that you had company over you said you were spending a quiet night alone."

"And you didn't take the Benz in the driveway as a sign?"

"Don't get sassy," She says squinting her eyes. "So how was it?"

"Oh, we are not doing that today."

She shrugs her shoulders and takes a drink of her orange juice. My mother was not shy, and she definitely did not mind asking my sister and I twenty-one questions about our sex lives or giving us advice and tips to use in the bedroom either. Which still to this day creeps me out but then again, she wouldn't be my mother if she wasn't poking and prodding. I'd probably think something was wrong with her and have Brendan scan her brain for me if she didn't.

"Good morning ladies," Brendan said walking into the kitchen and over to me leaning in and kissing me on the cheek.

"Good morning doctor," my mom said in a voice that made me roll my eyes at her.

"You can call me Brendan, Mrs. Wilmore," He says with a huge smile on his face and I can tell that he notices my mother's being flirtatious.

"Well, I'm going to run along and let you kids get back to your little romp in the sheets."

"Mom," I shout.

She laughs then leans in and kisses me on the cheek before saying goodbye and heading out of the house. I tell you that old woman is getting more and more outspoken with age.

Chapter Eleven

Brendan

Last night while we were at one of those restaurants where the kids can eat, and play Jasmine asked her mom if the name Dr. Yummy, is my nickname. Because she'd overheard her mom say it to aunt Natalie. Needless to say, the blush on Marissa's cheeks were confirmation enough that she and her sister had discussed our late-night romp, as her mother called it when she walked in on us. Josh and I hit it off as well even though I wasn't sure about how hard I was going to have to work to win him over, but once we started talking about football and realized we were fans of the same team that was the start of a special bonding moment.

I'd taken them to my house to hang out after dinner and to watch movies on the big screen in my theater room and let's just say princess Jasmine was all too thrilled she called it a castle. The kids had fallen asleep during the movie and we carried them to the guest room and tucked them in since it was late, and I really didn't want her to go. I'd woken up early and ran out to get breakfast for Marissa and the kids. At first, I'd thought about making something for them, but cooking is not really something that I'm very skilled in.

"Good morning Mr. Brendan," Josh said his body hiding behind the wall.

"Good morning," I respond offering him a warm smile and waving him over.

95

He walks over and takes a seat at the breakfast bar and crosses his arms in front of him tapping his fingers on the countertop. I go back to placing the food on to each plate, but he lets out a sigh and I place the spoon back into the container and look over at him.

"Looks like you have something on your mind. Do you want to talk about?" I ask watching his face closely.

"Well—," he begins, sitting back on the stool. "I was just wondering if you and my mom are going to be like boyfriend and girlfriend."

"What did your mother tell you we were?" I questioned.

"She just calls you her friend, but I know that it has to be something more than that." He says, looking up and meeting my gaze.

"And what makes you say that?"

"Because she gets all googly-eyed whenever your around and she talks about you a lot mostly with my aunt Nat and her friends."

"Oh yeah," I reply, and he shakes his head yes.

I was getting some very good intel from Josh when Jasmine came running into the kitchen bouncing up onto the stool beside her brother and smiling at us. She reached over and grabbed one of the grapes from the fruit bowl and popped it in her mouth then rubbed her hands on her tummy as her brother and I watched in amusement.

"Good morning gorgeous," I say kissing Marissa on the cheek as she gives me a side hug.

96

"Morning! Something smells good," she says looking down at the food spread out on the counter.

"I ordered breakfast. How about we all go into the front room and eat breakfast while we watch some cartoons."

Jasmine screams and jumps down from the stool and runs towards the living room as the rest of us grab the plates and follow behind her. I sit with my arm around Marissa watching her and the kids as they focus their attention on the cartoon that I'd never heard or seen before, and I couldn't help but to think, why hadn't I ever wanted this for myself. I mean I wanted to be a family with Nia and travel the world, but I'd never imagined us having kids or having moments like this one or last night. But now that I have I don't want to go back I want to have these kinds of moments every day for the rest of my life and I want to have them with Marissa and her two beautiful kids and maybe even add one more.

We'd spent the whole morning in front of the television until I got an emergency call from Janice, so I got dressed and then drove Marissa and the kids home and headed over to the hospital.

After checking on my patient and talking to the on-call physician at the hospital I headed back home and grabbed my duffel bag and a few things for the gym and left out again to meet Jamison at the gym. When I arrived, Jamison was already in full beast mode running his last mile on the treadmill as I approached him.

"Well, it's about time you showed up. I thought I was going to have to send out the cavalry," he joked grabbing his towel off the side and wiping his face.

"Very funny," I say with a sarcastic laugh. "I'll be back in a minute man I'll meet you at the bench press."

I head into the locker room and change then meet back up with him and we go to work lifting weights. A couple of young guys come over and join us and it quickly turns into a dick measuring contest as they challenge us to see who could lift the most and there is no need to ask who won that matchup. Those young boys couldn't lift half of what I and my man Jamison were pressing, it was pretty much half of their body weight combined.

We decided to go over to the juice bar and take a break and grab something to eat.

"So, what happen did you decide to sleep in late." He asks, taking a drink of his water.

"No, I was kind of preoccupied this morning."

"Oh yeah, was she hot?" He says wiggling his eyebrows and I couldn't help but laugh at the ridiculous expression on his face.

"Hell. Yes. She is smoking!" I reply.

"Nice," he chuckles and takes a bite out of his sandwich then begins talking with his mouth full. "Does she have a sister?"

"Uh, yeah, she does actually." I say, "and she also has two kids," I tell him, and his mouth falls open as a surprised look appears on his face.

"Wait—what?" He says wiping off his mouth and leaning back in his seat.

I tell him about Jasmine and Josh and how amazing they are and how great their mom is. It's really no secret everyone knows that I've always shied away from women who have kids because I've never really wanted kids of my own, but now I can say that something changed in me the very moment that I meet Marissa and her children. So, with that said I've gotten used to the reaction of my friends and colleges being surprised at the mere mention of me dating a woman that has two kids.

We hit the showers, get dressed, and then head over to the bar to grab a few beers before we head home for the evening.

"So, how are things going with your ex-wife?"

He huffs and says, "It's going, man."

I look over at him and see notice the sad expression that now replaced the smile that was on his face and I immediately regret bringing it up. She must really be giving him a tough time with the custody case although I really don't understand why she felt the need to have a judge make the decision on when he should be allowed time with his daughter. Jamison is a great father and he loves the hell out of his little girl, but I suppose she's doing it out of spite.

I change the conversation to a lighter subject to kind of ease the tension that was growing. The bar was crowded and that wasn't unusual it is a Saturday night and there's a football game on tonight, so everyone has come to watch it on the big screen. A cute blonde and a very sexy brunette walk up beside Jamison to order drinks and a smile spreads across the brunette's face when our eyes connect until the bartender calls out to her asking what she'd like to drink. I nudge Jamison's arm and nod my head towards the two ladies and he quickly straightened up in his seat and his lips part into a small smile.

The blonde turns to face a smiling Jamison and smiles back at him and after the bartender place their drinks in front of them they hesitate and linger around for a moment while the blonde waits for Jamison to say something. But he tenses up and doesn't say anything, he just sits there fiddling his beer bottle in his hand, so I knew that I was going to have to take the lead on this one.

"Hey, how are you ladies doing this evening?"

"Great," they say in unison then look at each other and giggle.

"We'd be a lot better if ya'll join us for drinks." The brunette says, walking over and standing beside me leaning in and pressing her perfect C-cup breast into my arm.

And I don't know if it was the lustful look in her eye or that cute accent that made my dick twitch, but she definitely has that something that makes me want to pin her tiny frame to my California king and fuck the shit out of her. When my eyes met her gaze again she looks at me with a knowing smile on her face almost like she could tell exactly what I was thinking.

We find ourselves a quiet table in the back but still close enough to see the big screen and quiet enough to spark a conversation with the two young women. The brunette whose name is Chasity, is kind of quiet but the blonde, whose name is Laney, is the more outspoken one. Which didn't really shock me all that much because most blondes are chatty. They told us that they both worked as office assistants at a very successful law firm, but Chasity was only working as an assistant until she passes her bar exams which she'll be taking in a few weeks.

"So, what is that the two of you do for a living?" Chasity asks placing her hand on my knee.

"We're doctors. I actually have my own practice in the city."

"Really," Laney says excitedly.

"I sure wish my doctor looked like you," Chasity cuts in.

She slides her hand up my thigh and her hand brushes over the bulge in my pants and her eyes go wide for a moment and glances over at me her cheeks flushed and a playful smile dancing on her lips. Usually, that would have been all the confirmation I needed, and we would have been out the door and, on our way, back to my place. But after a few more beers I decided to call it a night, I paid our tab then met Jamison and the ladies outside of the bar. After saying our goodbyes, I watched as Jamison and Laney climbed into a cab and disappear into the evening traffic. I waited with Chasity until her ride arrives and then for my driver Ahmad to arrive.

When he pulls up to the curb I hop inside and get comfortable glad to be inside the warmth of the car because it had gotten colder. Before we parted ways, Chasity gave me her number, but I don't plan on using it. I just wanted to create an opening for Jamison so that he could get with the blonde because he really needs it. With all the stress of the divorce and custody hearings lately a good release will do him good.

I take out my phone and check for any missed calls or text, but my phone was dry and has been all day. I felt a ting of disappointment settle in my gut as I stared down at my phone I haven't spoken to Marissa since I dropped them off at home this morning and strangely she's been on my mind all day and I couldn't help but wonder what her and the kids were up to, but it seemed a little late to call. When we pulled up to my front door said goodnight to Ahmad and headed inside and got settled and ready for bed.

****

I'd woken up with my dick hard as steel after dreaming about Marissa all night. I wanted to call her up and have her come over and help me take care of it but instead, I settled for a quick release during my morning shower. My commute to work was the best there was a wreck that caused one whole side of the road to be closed off and on top of that, the holiday traffic is getting more and more ridiculous as Christmas nears.

I haven't thought much about the holidays really, so maybe I'll go and visit my parents who are still in my hometown of Knoxville, TN. I'm sure they'll be surprised and grateful that I made the trip home for the holidays since I haven't been back in a couple of years. Nia was never big on celebrating and that goes for anything Christmas, Thanksgiving, New Year day, birthdays, etc. So, every year we pretty much stayed home and treated the day as if it was just another day to mark off our calendars.

"What's up, man?" Jamison asks popping his head into my office just as I'd taken my seat and sat my coffee mug on the desk.

"Hey, nothing much ready to get my day started." I began, "You seem to be quite the chipper chimp this morning, dare I ask what's gotten into you?"

"Laney, that's what!" he says coming over and taking a seat in front of my desk.

"The blonde from the bar?" I ask surprised, yawing and picking up my mug to take a sip.

"Correct," He smiles a goofy grin. "After we left the bar we went back to my place and let's just say we didn't come up for air until 5 am this morning."

"Impressive," I nod to him. "So, are you thinking that this might turn out to be more than a weekend fling?" I ask a bit curious.

Don't get me wrong I was happy that he'd finally pulled himself out of the trenches and finally got some good gush, but I also didn't want him to rush into anything or mistake a good lay for something else.

"Dr. Marston," one of the nurses says stepping into my office getting both of our attention. "Your patient is ready, sir."

"Thanks, Mal," he says with a nod and she disappeared from the doorway. "Alright man, we'll finish up later."

He heads off to tend to his patient and I dive into the paperwork that was waiting for me on my desk. I'd gotten my desk halfway cleared off when the nurse let me know that my first appointment this morning had arrived, so I grabbed my coat and follow her down to the exam room.

I'd gotten through most of the day without my mind being filled with thoughts of Marissa, but just as I take my seat back in my office where it's quiet and there are no distractions my mind began to wander. I picture her beautiful curly hair falling around her face while she sleeps and the way her eyes sparkle whenever I make her laugh, and the flush of her cheeks every time she gets aroused but tries to hide the way that she's feeling.

103

"Your so obvious," I hear Janice say, standing in the doorway to my office.

"And what does that suppose to mean?" I ask, shaking the thoughts from my mind.

"You've been mooning around here like a love-sick teenager for the last couple of weeks." She laughs walking over and sitting a stack of folders on my desk. "I'm going to go out on a limb and assume that things are going really well with your new squeeze."

I chuckle and shake my head at her choice of words. "I have no idea what you're talking about, Janice."

"Sure," she says in a sarcastic tone as she laughs.

I hate to admit it but she's right. But I can't help but smile every time that I think of her, and I think about her a lot. I know that it's showing, and others are taking notice as well especially Janice. I go through the files that Janice brought me and sign all the necessary documentation before returning them to her so that she could file them before we closed for the day.

I go back into my office and check my phone again for any new calls, texts, or voicemails and I was pleased to see a text from Marissa and I quickly opened it taking my seat back behind my desk.

Marissa: Hey you! I haven't heard from you since Saturday, I hope everything is ok. Things at the restaurant have been crazy but if you're not busy tonight maybe you can stop by for dinner. Just let me know!

I smile down at the screen as I read over the text then I type out a quick reply accepting her invite to dinner. I sit my phone back on my desk and turn back to my laptop so that I could finish up and then head out so that I can stop by the house before I make my way to Marissa's.

Chapter Twelve

Marissa

"Do you really want a relationship with the first guy you've banged after your drought?" Belia asks stepping off the treadmill.

I give her a side eye glance as I walk over and grab a towel from the stand and wipe my face. It wasn't like I'd planned to fall for Brendan, hell I hadn't even planned on sleeping with him, or have him meet my kids and have an instant connection with them. Josh likes when he's around, and I think it's mainly because he likes having another male around and Jasmine, well she'd taken to him instantly and hasn't stopped talking about him ever since.

We go over to the bikes and choose the two that were next to each other and continued our workout. Belia would glance over at me and I tried to ignore her, but I could feel her stare burning a hole in the side of my face.

"Look I don't know," I begin, "He's a really nice guy and my kids like him a lot plus we haven't talked about where things are going from here anyways. Maybe awesome mind-blowing sex maybe the only thing we ever have."

"Would that be such a terrible thing?" she glances over at me with a questionable look on her face. "Omgosh! Your falling for him, aren't you?"

"No—NO!" I stutter.

"You are!" She shouts causing everyone around us to turn and look in our direction. "You've gone and fallen in love with Dr. Hottie."

"Shh…" I whisper, "Quiet down Belia. He's a member here as well, geez just tell all of my business why don't you."

She shrugs her shoulder at me with a smirk on her face and gets off her bike. Her phone rings just as she reached for her water and after she looked at the screen she held up her finger and walked towards the lobby to take the call. Why does my friend have to be so nosey and loud?

"Hey, I have to go there's an emergency at the office and we're going to finish this conversation." She says giving me a quick hug then heads towards the door.

"No, we won't," I call out to her as she jogs towards the door.

I grab my things and head out to my car and slide into the driver's seat. I take out my phone and send Brendan a quick text, I hadn't heard from him since Saturday morning when he'd driven us home and rushed off to take care of one of his patients. I invited him over for dinner and he accepted which put a huge smile on my face that has actually been happening a lot lately and it's not so bad. I'm happy to have a reason to smile, I'm happy to have a man in my life that makes me want to smile again.

I stop and grab a few groceries before I headed home. I pulled into the driveway and put the car in park the kids were in the front yard with my sister and my mother and I take a breath and exhale before I get out the car. I didn't know that my mother was going to be stopping by today and I really wish that she had told me before I'd invited Brendan to dinner.

"Hey Chica," my sister calls as I walk up the sidewalk.

"Mommy, mommy," Jasmine yells. "Look at what Auntie Nat taught me to do." She said turning a flip and landing on her bottom.

"Great job sweetheart," I say smiling at her. "Hey, you boys want to grab the groceries from the car for me," I ask Josh and his friend who was sitting on the front porch.

"Sure mom," Josh replies.

"Hello darling," my mother says giving me a quick embrace.

"Hi mom," I say kissing her on the cheek.

The boys run over to the car and grab the bags and take them into the house then run back out the door reclaiming their spots and grabbing their game systems. My mother and my sister follow me into the house and join me in the kitchen as I began to put up the groceries and pull out the things that I need for dinner.

"Need any help," my mother asks.

"No thank you. I think I can manage." I say in a flat tone.

My sister looks back and forth between the two of us confused by the tension that was in the room bouncing around. I was still feeling some kind of way about my mom walking in on Brendan and me as well as her little commentary afterward and she knew it.

She chuckled then turned to face my sister. "Oh, your sisters just upset that I walked in on her and that hunky doctor sweating the sheets the other day."

I slam the door to the fridge shut then turned to look at the both of them crossing my arms in front of my chest. My sister giggle then looks at me with a surprised look on her face before clapping her hands spinning around in the stool that she was sitting in.

"You're not funny," I say in a hard tone and my mother winks at me.

"Alright sis," my sister cheers. "I knew you had it in you, now tell us how it was?"

"What makes you think I want to talk about my sex life with my mother in the room?"

"Oh, please sex is what got you here," my mom huffs.

"Geez—mom I don't want to hear about you and dad's sex sessions," I said cringing at the thought.

Sometimes I swear that I was adopted because my mother and my sister are like two peas in a pod and I feel like I'm the outcast that was conceived from a whole other strain of DNA.

"I'm going to take a shower can the two of you finish up please?"

"Of course, darling."

"And mom can you please stop with the comedy sex banter Brendan's coming over for dinner tonight." I plead with my mother. "And you, you behave as well." I say pointing a finger at my sister and she throws up her hands.

109

I shower and slide on a pair of jeans and a plain black t-shirt then pull my hair into a loose bun and head back downstairs. The thought to call Brendan and tell him that something came up had crossed my mind, but before I could fully decide on it there was a heavy knock at the door and my heart began to thud against my chest.

"I got it," my sister called out to me from the living room.

"Thanks," I replied happy that it wasn't my mom who'd gotten up to open the door.

I pull the glass pan from the stove and set it on the counter as I listened to the voices in the foyer get closer to the kitchen and they stop just as Brendan walks into the kitchen. My gosh, I can't believe how responsive my body is to this man even the masculine smell of his cologne gets my blood rushing and my heart pounding. His lips pull into a smile and I'm sure that it's because he's noticed the flush of my cheeks which is starting to get embarrassing, but I just can't seem to control my body whenever he's around.

"Hello gorgeous," He says softly walking over sliding his arms around my waist pulling me into him and kissing my neck.

"Hi handsome," I say with a huge smile on my face.

I turn in his arms and press my lips to his kissing him slowly, lifting my arms and wrapping them loosely around his neck.

"Eww," we hear a tiny voice say.

We look over at Jasmine standing in the doorway with her tongue sticking out and her face scrunched up like she'd just eaten something sour. I laugh, and release Brendan and he walks over and scoops Jasmine up in his arms and starts giving her little kisses on her cheek and she starts to scream and wiggle in his arms trying to get free. My heart swells as I watch him and how great he is with my children and I can't help but wonder if this is how things were supposed to turn out for us because it just feels so right.

"Dinner's ready you guys," I call out to them and everyone enters the dining room and takes a seat.

Everyone was enjoying themselves and for once my mother didn't have me clawing at the table because of her colorful sense of humor. Once we'd finished with dinner the kids ate their snacks then ran off to their rooms to get ready for bed. Once they were showered and ready to be tucked in I meet them in their rooms.

"Mommy is it ok if Mr. Brendan tucks me in tonight?" Jasmine asks standing at the end of the stairs.

"Hey Brendan," I call for him to come over. "Princess Jasmine here would like for you to tuck her in. Do you think you can handle that?" I say with a wink.

"Please," Jasmine says giving him an irresistible pouty face.

"Oh… alright," he gives her a warm smile at her then scoops her into his arms and heads up the stairs.

My mom and sister help me clean up the kitchen put the dishes away before leaving out. And as soon as the house was empty and quiet I grabbed a glass of wine for myself and a beer for Brendan and we made our way to the living room and got comfortable on the sofa in front of the tv.

"I like your family," He said with a grin, "Your mom is quite something, she reminds me of my receptionist Janice."

111

"Well, just wait until you meet my dad." I joke.

He chuckles and then picks up his beer taking a swig from the bottle then places it back on the tables then shifts himself so that he's facing me. I felt like putty every time his gaze met mine and for those few moments, we would get lost in each other.

"Marissa," He said, and I look away blinking a couple of times, "I think that we should talk about where all of this is going. I mean what are we doing, is this just going to be about sex or do you see a future for us?"

I swallow hard and look up at him then I take a deep breath and remain quiet for a second before answering his question. Honestly, I didn't know but I do know that it isn't only sex because I do feel something for him, but I don't really know how to express my feelings and I don't want to move too fast and scare him away.

"I don't know Brendan. I mean do we really need to put a title to things?"

"Yes, I think that we do," he says moving his arm from around me and putting some distance between us which let me know that we'd reached that point where we need to make a decision. "Josh ask me over the weekend if I was going to be your boyfriend."

"Omgosh, what did you say?"

"I didn't say anything, Marissa. I didn't know what to say so I told him that it was something he needed to talk with you about."

I sigh heavily and run my hands through my hair. "Maybe this was a mistake letting them meet you so soon. I probably should've given this a little more thought then I did before having a strange man come around."

"Wow," He says placing his hands together and holding them to his mouth. "Ok, so I think I'm going to go ahead and uh—go."

"Oh, no. Brendan. Please, I didn't mean it like that I—," I pause and reach out to place my hand on his shoulder, but I stop myself.

He stands and silently walks towards the front door grabbing his coat from the closet and then walking out the door. I place my hands over my mouth realizing what I'd just said and how it must have sounded, and it takes everything in me to stop the tears that were filling my eyes from falling. I jump up from the couch and rush to the front door and run out, I catch him just ask he's opening the car door to get inside.

"Brendan. Please wait!" I call out to him. "I'm so sorry I shouldn't have said that or said it in that way."

"Marissa, I really like you and to be honest I could see myself falling in love with you, but I don't want to play games. If you're not ready for something more or you need time to figure it out that's fine just tell me, and I'll give you that space and time."

I wanted to throw caution to the wind and throw myself into his arms and hope for the best, but I can't. I have more than myself to think about in this situation and what if it doesn't work out? How will that affect my children they've already taken to him and my son is starting to look up to him as well as, opening up to him, and I don't think he or Jasmine could take losing another father figure.

"I'm sorry Brendan but I'm just not ready," I say, and he takes a deep breath and he shut his eyes then he exhaled sadness clouding his features.

He rubs his hand over my cheek and lifts my lips to his and kisses me softly. I close my eyes and pressed my lips to his feeling the words that were unsaid in that one kiss. He pulls away and fakes a smile before getting into his car and pulling out of the driveway as a tear streamed down my cheek and in a matter of seconds he was gone, and I felt my body get weak as the tears began to really flow.

I turned and walked back into the house and locked the door behind me, turning off all the lights and heading up to my room. I fell onto the bed and curled myself into a fetal position and wept into my pillow and I fell asleep.

Chapter Thirteen

Brendan

I tossed and turned all night and woke up feeling as though the world had come crashing down all around me. Last night Marissa called me a stranger and said that she'd regretted having me around her children and when she said it was like someone ripped through my chest and was squeezing my heart so tight that it erupted in my chest. Everything was going so well, and her kids adore me so why is she being this way, why is she pulling away from me?

I called the office and asked Jamison and Dawn to split up my patients that were scheduled for appointments today so that Janice wouldn't have to spend the whole afternoon rescheduling appointments. I needed to take the day off and get my mind right, so I decided to mope around the house in my pajama bottoms all day instead of going into the office and not getting anything done or giving my full attention to my patients.

After running 3 miles on the treadmill I showered and made myself lunch eating it in front of the tv while I caught up on some of the latest movies that'd been released. I started to doze off when my cell phone rang, I wasn't really in the mood to talk to anyone but thought against not answering it just in case it was a real emergency.

"Hello," I answered.

"Hello, my sweet boy," I hear my mother say as her voice came across the line.

"Hey ma," I reply with a small smile.

"I got your message this morning. I'm so excited that your coming to spend Christmas with us this year and so is your father." She beamed, and I could hear the smile in her voice.

I missed my mom and her loving caring nature especially at a times like this when I'm feeling really down in the dumps. She always knows just the right words to say to get me out of a funk no matter the situation and her timing was perfect because I really need some sound advice from someone other than Janice who would only tell me that she told me so.

"You sound a little down, is everything ok?" My mother asks.

"Yes, everything is fine. I'm just tired." I say not really wanting to get into my situation over the phone I'd rather wait until we're face to face.

I talk to my mother for a while longer then my dad for about an hour before we said our goodbyes and I ended the call tossing my phone onto the couch and kicking up my feet.

Two glasses of scotch later and I was feeling more upbeat now that my mind was foggy and sitting home alone moping was beginning to get boring. The brunette from the bar came to mind so I went to my room and got the napkin from my pocket that she'd written her number on and dialed the number. Three rings later an excited voice came across the line.

"Hello."

"Hey, Chasity, this is Brendan. We met at the bar a few nights ago."

"Hey, yeah. How are you?" she asks.

"I'm great. How about yourself?"

"I'm awesome now that you've called."

"Well, how about I make your night even better by coming to keep you company."

She giggles, "I guess that would be ok. I'll text you my address."

"Great, I'll see you soon."

I hang up and head into my closet, grabbing a pair of jeans, a sweatshirt, and quickly get dressed. If Marissa wants to live her life alone then that was her choice, but I wasn't going to wait around for her to change her mind I'd already lost seven years of my life with a woman that wasn't sure if I was what she wanted, and I wasn't going to do it again.

I check my phone for Chasity's text as I walk out to the car and climbed inside. I punched in the address into my GPS before I pulled out of the garage and was on my way. I'm hoping that once I arrive there's very little small talk because I'd rather skip the small talk and get right to my hand gripping her ass while I'm taking her from behind.

fifteen minutes later I pull in front of a two-story townhouse and parked behind the lime green beetle that was parked by the curb. When I reached the door, I pressed the doorbell and heard the chiming sounds behind the closed door. A few seconds later the door slowly opened, and I was shocked that she was standing in the doorway with a sexy piece of lingerie that hugged her curves in all the right ways.

117

"Hey, come in," she said taking my hand and pulling me in the door closing and locking it behind us.

"You look really—"

"I know," she says cutting me off with a wink. "I'm glad that you finally called me."

"So am I," I say to myself as I follow her lead.

We walk into the room and she pushes me onto the bed, unbuttons my jeans, and pulls out my cock slowly kneeling down in front me. She begins stroking my manhood and I stiffen in her hand with every stroke. I close my eyes and tilt my head back a little as a low groan escapes me.

"Impressive," She whispers and lower mouths to my hard cock and licks the tip, slowly circling her tongue around it while she looks me in the eye.

Fuck she looks so hot and I love that she's not shy or afraid to look me in the eye while she takes all of my dick into her mouth deep throating it, licking my balls and rolling her tongue as she moves back up. The pleasure starts to build more and more each time I hit the back of her throat and it feels so good that my hips thrust forward, and my dick pushes deeper into her hot wet mouth.

"Ah, fuck," I shout.

"Yes, baby give your cum. I want to taste you." She says before taking me back into her mouth and moving her head up and down faster.

I feel the pressure begin to build and I run my finger through her hair grabbing a fist full of it taking control and fuck her hot wet mouth until my dick spasms and I erupt filling her mouth with my cum. She sits up and wipes her mouth with the back of her hand and smiles a really seductive smile with her face flushed and her lips now a cherry red and a little swollen from sucking me off.

"You taste fucking amazing," she said licking her fingers as she stood to her feet.

I lean forward and smack her on the ass, pulling her close, and wrapping my arms around her waist lifting her up and spinning around and tossing her on the bed. She gasps and does this little cute giggle that made my dick perk up once again ready for round two.

"You're a naughty girl."

"I like being naughty and I also like bad boys, are you a bad boy Dr. Hopkins?" She says in the most intoxicating voice I'd ever heard and the way she said my name mad me hard as a rock.

"You tell me," I reply flipping her over onto her belly and smacking her hard across her ass and she lets out a loud moan before I smack the other side and watch her ass cheeks turn a nice shade of red.

I lift her ass in the air and spread her legs, kissing the places where my hands had landed before slowly moving my face to her pussy. I let my tongue trace over the imprint of her pussy before sliding her panties to the side and parting her lips and sucking on her clit then sucking it into my mouth.

"Yes…" she moans.

"Do you like that."

"Yes…" she cries out.

119

I remove my mouth and slide a finger inside of her and slowly move in and out of her, she begins to rock back onto my hand matching my rhythm and I could feel her walls tighten around my fingers, so I pull them out of her.

"Not yet," I say standing up and taking the condom out of my pocket, shaking out of my jeans, and kicking them to the side before taking my place behind her again.

I rub the head of my penis over her slit opening her up then slowly easy my hard-on into her opening and she gasp, and her body stiffens as she fists the sheet.

"You're really fucking tight."

"And you're really fucking big." She says gasping for breath as I pound into her.

I thrust forward fucking her hard from behind gripping her waist tight and loving the sound of her ass bouncing back on to my dick. I was so filled with hunger and need that I pushed into her deeper and harder each time as screamed my name telling me that she was about to cum. Her walls tightened around my dick and I could feel her pussy flex and she cried out as her orgasm took over and ripped through her over and over again all the while sending me over the edge. I continue to thrust forward slowing down each time as we ride out our individual orgasms before I slowly pull out of her and fall onto the bed beside her panting.

After several minutes of silence, catching our breath, and regaining function of our bodies she rolls over and scoot over towards me and laying across my chest and I stroke her back.

"That. Was. AMAZING!" She says, her lips turned up into a small smile.

"So, do I meet the criteria of a bad boy?"

"Oh, that you do!" She laughs and leans forward and kisses me.

I close my eyes and lean into the kiss pulling her on top of me. Her breast pressed into my chest and I could feel her erect nipples pushing into me. For some reason, Marissa crosses my mind and a wave of uneasiness came over me as I thought about how she would feel if she knew about my sexcapade with Chasity so soon after our split, if we can even call it that. She pulls away and looks into my eyes studying my expression for a moment with a confused expression on her face as she sits up on top of me.

"Is something wrong?"

"Uh—no, I'm good," I say sitting up wrapping my arms around her. "Now, where were we?" I asked pulling her face towards mine and kissing her softly.

I don't know why I didn't make up some excuse and leave right after we'd finished maybe because I didn't want to go back to that big house and spend the rest of the night alone. I slid my arm out from under Chasity and sat up on the side of the bed taking a deep breath and running my hands over my face before getting up and quietly searching for my jeans. I slipped them on and walked towards the door slowly opening it and creeping out and closing it behind me. I walked down the hall until I reached the kitchen then went over to the fridge and opened it looking for something to drink.

It wasn't very full but there were a couple of bottles of water on the door, so I grabbed one and shut it hoping that she wouldn't mind. I twisted the cap and pressed the bottle to my lips taking a long drink of the water when the lights flickered on and I turned around finding a slightly older woman standing there with her robe on and eyeing me like a piece of meat. I could feel her gaze move up and down my body stopping on my crotch before our eyes met again.

"My, my, Christmas sure did come early this year." She said as her lips parted into a small smile.

"I'm sorry if I woke you I was just getting a bottle of water," I replied holding up the bottle of water that was now half empty.

"It's all good. I'm guessing that you're here visiting my niece, Chasity."

"Uh, yeah I am. My names Brendan it's nice to meet you—" I say pausing and waiting for her name as I hold out my hand for her.

"Belia," she says then walks closer to me taking the hand that I had extended to her shaking it then brushing past me.

I finish the rest of the water in the bottle then throw it in the trash and say goodnight to Belia before heading back up to Chasity's room and climbing back into the bed. I wish I would have known that she had told me that her aunt was visiting or staying with her so that I would have known not to go walking around the house half naked. I laid back on the pillow and got comfortable closing my eyes and before I knew it I was fading into the darkness.

The alarm on my phone startled me and I jump up straight in the bed looking around the room I'd forgotten where I was for a moment. I got up from the bed and walked over grabbing my jeans from the floor and removing my phone turning off the alarm. I rub my hands through my hair and then find my clothes and slip them on along with my shoes before I walk out the bedroom to find the bathroom. After I take a leak I head down the hall towards the kitchen where I heard voices and laughter, Chasity and her aunt were sitting at the nook in the corner of the kitchen drinking coffee and talking.

"Well, good morning handsome," Chasity says getting up and coming over to kiss me.

"Good morning ladies," I reply looking over in Belia's direction and she winks at me and offers me a smile as she blows into her cup. "I have to get going I don't want to keep my patients waiting."

"Ok, I'll be waiting for your call doc." She says before turning around to walk away and I smack her on her ass and she giggles.

I caught the look on her aunt's face when she Chasity mentioned doctor but I'm not sure why the questionable look. I shake the thought and head out of the door and over to my car climbing inside and pulling away from the townhouse. I need to get home and take a quick shower before I headed into the office for the day I mean I would have brought a change of clothes and kept them in the car, but I hadn't planned on being there overnight.

I finished up with my last patient of the afternoon then headed out to grab lunch from the burger joint down the street from the office. The double cheeseburger, extra fries, and milkshake that I ordered were probably going to give me a hell of a case of heartburn later but at the moment I didn't care because I was starving. I'd skipped breakfast so that I wouldn't be late this morning and as soon as I walked in the door my patient was seated in the exam room waiting for me, so I dove right into work.

Snow had begun to fall, and it had lightly covered the ground by the time I'd come out of the restaurant, so I quickly got in the car. When I got back to the office I had Janice call to make sure that the sidewalk and the parking lot was going to be salted by the end of business day. I'm sure by morning there will be a lot more snow and I want everything to be easy going for my patients.

Chapter Fourteen

Marissa

BRRR!

The temperature had dropped since this morning when I'd come to the restaurant and there was now a foot of snow covering the ground. I said one last goodbye to my staff and let out a slow steady breath as I wrapped my scarf around my neck, pull my hood over my head, and rushing out to my car. I can picture Jasmine standing in the window jumping up and down looking out at the snow with excitement oozing from her and I'm sure Josh is going to be happy about getting a snow day. I'm sure they'll call it off seeing as to how they haven't started on the roads just yet.

I pull into the driveway and shut off the car and reaching into the backseat to gather my things before I get out of the car. The lights were out so I'm guessing that Nat actually got the kids to go to bed on time for once in her life. She's always liked playing the cool aunt and letting them do whatever they wanted until she realized that they saw that as her being a pushover. I stepped out of the car and a cool breeze brushed past me giving me the chills causing my body to shiver and shake

"Hey there supermom," Belia said jogging across the street and up to the car reaching for the bags in my hand. "Let me help you with that."

"Thanks," I smiled at her then turned and closed the car door.

125

I flipped the keys in my hand trying to get to the right one so that I could open the front door when it swings open. Natalie was flushed, looked a little out of breath, and her hair was messy, an after-sex kind of messy.

"Hey," she says breathlessly. "Your home earlier than usual tonight."

"Uh—yeah business is slow probably because of the snow," I say walking past her and noticing the guy from the gym stretched out on my sofa and I quickly jerk my head back around to Natalie.

Belia walks in behind me and looks over at him and raises her eyebrow at Natalie. I shake my head and walk towards the kitchen sitting my keys on the breakfast bar and my bags in the chair before turning back to Natalie just as she reached the kitchen.

"Ok, before you say anything we weren't doing what you think. He leaned in and kissed me and things kind of got a little heated." She said then paused as she watched my face ball up.

I hold up my hand to her and shake my head at her before taking off my coat and throw it over the chair. She knows that I don't like her bringing men into my house especially a man that she barely even knows and bumping and grinding on my sofa is overstepping.

"He's kind of hot, you know, in a bad boy kind of way," Belia says and I give her a side eye glance and roll my eyes and they both giggle.

"What if your niece or nephew would've walked in on the two of you?" I ask.

"Calm down Marissa it's not like we were naked or anything," She snorts.

"I'm very calm, but you should know better and I've asked you not to bring stranger men into my house."

"He's not a stranger," she snickers, and I give her a questionable look, "What? I've been seeing him for almost three months now."

I turn to her my eyes wide, "Really?"

"Uh, yeah! Why are you acting so surprised?" She asked with a confused look on her face but both Belia and I ignore her question.

I love my sister, but I will admit that I'm shocked that she's stuck with a guy for more than two weeks. My sister has never been one to keep a man longer than a couple of weeks to her commitment issues that she claims to have when it comes to settling down with one man. For some reason she seems to always find something wrong with them when things get serious.

"Speaking of hot hunky men how are things going with you and Dr. Handsome?" Belia asks sliding into the chair at the end breakfast bar.

"It's not." I reply with a long sigh, "I kind of said something that was hurtful and then he was asking me about taking the next step and I freaked out and ended things."

"Oh, no. I'm sorry love." Belia said getting up from her chair and walking over giving me a big bear hug.

"I'm sorry sis," Natalie says coming over and joining in on the hug.

I grab a bottle of wine then we go into the living room and get comfortable on the sofa while Natalie walks her boyfriend out. I turn on some soft music and we have a glass of wine while having a little girl talk. Talking with the two of them and getting everything off my chest and listening to the advice they'd given me made me feel a lot better. I think tomorrow I'll make an appointment with my therapist maybe she can shed some light on why I'm having such a tough time letting go of Chandler and moving on with my life.

"You know I haven't started Christmas shopping yet. Maybe tomorrow the two of you can go with me and help me pick out a few things." Belia said.

"That sounds like fun. Plus, I still have a few last-minute things that I need to get for the kids and our parents. You can help me, sis, you can show me exactly what the kiddos are into now." Natalie adds.

"Let's do it!" I reply with a smile.

After saying our goodbyes, I walk them out and then I head up to my room and get ready for bed. I really miss Brendan coming around and I wish that he would call or maybe I should try calling him being that I'm the one that pushed him away, so I should probably make the first move. I pick up my phone and pull up his number letting my finger hover over the button for a second before clearing the screen and locking it back before throwing it onto the bed. Who was I fooling he probably doesn't want to talk to me, he's probably got some other woman that's occupying his mind and his time now that I'm out of the picture and I have no one to blame but myself.

****

I roll over on my side and tuck the pillow under my chin and take a deep breath. Tomorrow was a new a day and perhaps it would bring along a second chance for Brendan and me, that is if I can work up the nerve to call him and invite him over so that we can talk.

"Mommy, mommy, there's snow outside. Wake up!" Jasmine shouts jumping at the foot of the bed.

"Ok, I'm up—I'm up princess. Please stop jumping on the bed mommy has a headache." I say.

"Oh, no, mommy are you sick?" She asks. "Maybe we should call Dr. Brendan so that he can come help you feel better."

"No, sweetheart, I'm not sick. How about you and your brother go and get dressed so that you can go outside and build mommy a giant snowman."

"Ok, mommy." She replies as she jumps down from the bed and runs out of the room.

My head is pounding so I get up from the bed and go to the bathroom to grab some pain relievers before going to start breakfast. I go downstairs and stop in the foyer where I see my son helping his sister zipping up her coat then places her hat on her head.

"Hey kiddos, don't you want breakfast," I ask stopping by the door of the mudroom.

"No, ma'am. We've already had a bowl of cereal." Josh said smiling up at me.

"Oh, well, alright you guys make sure you put on your gloves," I tell them as I watch both of them run out the side door.

I go into the kitchen and see a note in my son's handwriting sitting in front of a mug of coffee on the counter that read, 'I hope I helped mom. I love you!'. I smile at the note and pick up the mug and slowly taking a sip. I close my eyes and enjoying the warmth as it fills my body. He's always been so helpful and warm natured something that he truly gets from his father.

I take my coffee into the front room and I sit on the sofa with my mug in hand and one of my favorite romance novels 'My Dream Man' and relax. I glance outside every now and again to check on the two of them and make sure that they're not getting into any mischief then turn my attention back to my book. I didn't notice myself dozing off while reading the book until I heard a loud scream and I jumped up from the couch and ran to the front door.

"What's wrong?" I call out to the kids.

"She hit me in the face with a snowball." Josh says wiping snow from his face.

Jasmine sitting on her knees in the snow laughing hysterically at her brother and I couldn't help but laugh along with her. Josh walks over to the porch his face balled up and his cheek a bright red.

"Alright you two it's time to come in and get warmed up," I say waving my hand towards them.

Josh walks into the house first and then Jasmine and I follow behind him. I shut the door and go into the kitchen to make us all some hot cocoa while they go and change into some dry clothes. I hand them their mugs once they get back downstairs and then we go into the living room and get settled on the sofa and watch a movie.

The doorbell rings and I head over to the door and opening it to let my mother and father in. Jasmine leaps off the sofa and runs into my father's arms while my mother gives me a quick embrace and then Josh. My father leans over and gives me a side hug while holding Jasmine in his other arm.

"Hello sweetheart," My father says kissing my cheek.

"Hey, dad!" I reply then release him.

"Grandpa, did you come to watch movies with us?" Jasmine shouts.

"Why yes, I did. Your grandmother and I are going to sit with you while your mom goes Christmas shopping with aunt Nat and Belia."

"Yay!" She yells as my father carries her into the front room and sets her down on the sofa.

I head up to my room to get dressed it's gotten colder since yesterday, so I grab a pair of skinny jeans, a sweater, and a pair of boots. I check myself in the mirror once more after pulling up my hair than head back downstairs to grab my scarf and coat.

"Hey sis, you ready to go?" Natalie asks.

"Hey, I didn't hear you two come in," I say stepping from the last step. "Let me grab my coat and then I'll be ready to go."

We say bye to my parents and the kids then head out to the car. I notice someone sitting in the car and then I realize that

131

it's Belia's niece sitting in the back seat of the car waving. I climb into the passenger seat and say hello to Chasity before buckling my seat belt. We ride to the mall singing along to the songs that were playing on the radio, well at least the ones we knew. We arrived at the mall and luckily found a parking spot that wasn't too far away from the entrance and then headed inside.

The mall was packed full of people shopping and laughing as they walked along. There was a Santa sitting close to the entrance where kids were getting their pictures taking and the line for that was massive. Some of the children were crying and others looked like they were trying to plan their escape from their parents. We went to a couple of kids stores and I helped Natalie pick out a couple of toys and some clothes for the kids and followed along while Belia got the things she needed. After a couple of hours of shopping we were all getting tired and very hungry, so we decided to go grab something to eat at the food court.

Nat and I grabbed pizza and Belia and her niece grabbed a couple of burgers and shakes then joined us at the table. Chasity's phone rings just as she sets her tray down on the table and takes her seat quickly pulling out her phone from her purse and answering it.

"Hey, you," she says as her face lights up and she holds up her hand to us while getting out of her seat.

We all shake our head and dig in I didn't really know Belia's niece all that well, but she seemed to be a lot like my sister and that really says a lot. The pizza was really greasy so after a few bites I pushed it to the side and grabbed my soda to wash down what little I had eaten. Of course, my sister grabbed it and finished it off for me because that was the one thing that I could rely on my sister to do was finish up my leftovers. It's always been that way since we were kids and you'd think she'd be as big as a house but nope she can eat a whole medium pizza on her own and never gain a pound.

A few minutes later Chasity joins us back at the table after her phone call. Her smile was so big that you'd think she just hit a jackpot on the lottery and when she notices us all staring at her, her cheeks blushed.

"What's got you all perked up," Belia asks.

"Nothing. I'm just happy, I'm always happy."

"Humph..." Belia replies with a look on her face. "That wouldn't happen to have been that hunky guy that was sneaking around in your kitchen the other night would it?"

Chasity's mouth falls open and she looks over at her aunt surprised. "Omgosh, I didn't know that you were at my place."

"I wasn't. I had only gotten there maybe an hour before." She smiled.

"Ah... that's so embarrassing."

"Oh, please. Your grown and you pay your own bills there is nothing to be ashamed of."

Chasity places her hand over her face and we all let out a little giggle and her face brightness more. We wait for her to finish her food and then we get going so that we can get the rest of our shopping done. I grab a gift for my parents and so does Nat and I'm not really sure how but somehow, we ended up in the lingerie store and I was being forced to purchase something sexy for my man candy. Even though I tried to talk my way out of it and convince them that I didn't need it they wouldn't back down.

"Come on you guys. Seriously. Who am I supposed to wear this for?" I asked stepping out of the fitting room.

They all started making howling noises and I turn to walk back into the fitting room but Belia grabs me and pulls me back.

"Oh, yeah. You sexy little MILF you." Chasity says and they all laugh.

"Sis, if you want to get that sexy piece of man candy back then this here will definitely do the trick," Natalie says snapping her finger at me.

"You look hot Marissa there is no way he's going to say no to all of that," Chasity says waving her hand over my curves.

"Ok, fine. I'll take it. Now can I put my clothes back on?"

"Sure, thing sexy mama," Natalie says smacking me on the ass and laughing.

I turn back and give her the finger before going back into the fitting room and closing the door. I stand in the mirror and give myself a once over thinking to myself 'damn, I really do look good'. Going to the gym had really paid off and I was back in shape and looking good once again and I also had a man that wanted to me, all of me. I change back into my clothes and then go out and pay for my things and we all head out to the car.

"So, my guy invited me out to the bar tonight. Do you all want to come?" Chasity asks.

134

"Mm. I don't know if I should," I say looking back and forth to each of them.

"Marissa you have really got to learn to live a little sis," Natalie said.

"Yeah Marissa, come on it'll be fun," Chasity says.

"Please..." Belia says with her lip out pouting.

I roll my eyes at them and sigh loudly, "Ok, Ok," I finally say.

Belia drops Nat and me back off at my house and then she and Chasity head home to drop off their things and to change into something a little sexier. Natalie insisted that we do the same, but I really didn't see the point of getting all dressed up just to go to a bar. She finally got the hint and stopped trying to persuade me and let it go, I freshened up my makeup and she did the same before we went back downstairs to wait on the two of them to get back. They pulled up an hour later and blew the horn and we headed out to the car and were off to the bar.

Chapter Fifteen

Brendan

I slide on my coat and zipping it up before I walked out of my office and out to the front of the office where everyone was waiting for me. They all grabbed their things and we went out to the parking lot together. I'd invited them out for drinks since we were closing earlier due to the weather and they agreed. Jamison decided to invite the blonde, so I figured what the hell and called up Chasity and ask her to come through with her friend and she accepted. Besides I'm in the mood to fill her up from behind while she screams out my name while she's clawing at the mattress.

I waited in my Navigator while they put their things in their cars and then got into the SUV one after the other until everyone was seated and ready to go. I drove down the block and found a spot that was slightly closer to the bar and parked by the curb. We all climb out of the Navigator and walked the rest of the way until we reached the bar. The music was loud and so were the people inside. You could hear the music clearly each time the door opened and that was before we'd even reached the entrance.

I'm guessing everyone had the same idea as we did this evening. We walk inside and look around for an empty table since there's too many of us to try and squeeze into a booth. Jamison spotted two empty tables towards the back and waved for us to follow him as he leads the way.

I take everyone's order and then head back up to the bar with Tish, one of my nurses, to grab the drinks for everyone. When we walked up to the bar to order the drinks all eyes were on me every lady at the bar was looking my way even the ones that were there with someone.

"You must get that a lot," Tish said shaking her head with a smile on her face.

"What?"

"The ladies," she said as she nods her head to each side. "You seem to be comfortable with all the attention."

"Yeah, after a while I stopped paying attention to it. That is unless I see something that I like." I say with a smile and she rolls her eyes at me and laughs.

"Ok, sex god! Grab the drinks so that we can get back to the table."

I chuckle and grab the rest of the drinks and follow behind her as she leads the way back to the table. I see the blonde sitting beside Jamison leaned in close to him laughing at whatever he was whispering in her ear and then I look over to their right and I see Chasity sitting beside her.

Chasity's eyes meet mine and she smiles at me before getting up from the table and coming over to hug me. I give a quick embrace while balancing the bottles of beer between my fingers then going over to the table and handing them over. I look across the table and I spot her aunt sitting next to Janice and she looks back at me with a closed lip smile and winks. Well, this night should be awkwardly interesting with her aunt here hanging out with us although she never mentioned bringing anyone so maybe her aunt is here waiting for someone.

"So, I had a great time the other night." Chasity leans over and whispers into my ear and I turn to look at her as her lips part into a smile.

"Well, if you enjoyed it that much then maybe we should go back to my place, and I can give you all of those things that you enjoyed all over again."

"Mm," she moans while biting her bottom lip.

She places her hand on my thigh and begins to move it up towards my manhood and my manhood immediately jumped to attention as she got closer. Right before her hand could get to the bulge that was now growing inside my jeans I heard someone say my name drawing my attention away from what was happening. Before I looked up I hadn't noticed that the voice that was calling out to me was a female until my eyes met her gaze.

"Marissa," I said softly leaning forward in my seat.

The table got quiet as everyone looked at the both of us confused not really understanding what was going on. The look on her face sent a sharp pain into my chest like someone had shoved a knife through it.

"You two know each other?" Chasity asks with a confused look on her face as she looked back and forth between the two of us.

"Yes—No. I mean I thought I did, but I guess I was wrong." She said then grabbed her coat and purse from the chair. "I'm sorry, I have to go." She said before turning and rushing towards the door.

"Marissa—," I call out to her, but she disappeared into the crowd. I stand up and grab my coat off the chair and slide it on so that I can go after her.

"Wait, where are you going?" Chasity asks but I ignore her and head for the door.

I push through the crowd and I finally make it to the door and walk out on to the sidewalk and look around searching for her. I catch a glimpse of her coat and start running in the direction that she's walking.

"Marissa," I call out to her, but she ignores me, so I jog a little faster. "Marissa, please, wait." I plead grabbing her arm once I reached her, but she jerks away from me.

"What do you want?" She says turning to face me and I could see the hurt and the anger all over her face.

"Would you please stop and talk to me."

"I have nothing to say to you, Brendan."

"And why is that, huh. Is it because I did what you told me to do and moved on?"

She looks at me and laughs before turning and walking back the opposite way back towards the bar. I turn and follow behind her hoping that she would eventually turn around or stop and say something, but she didn't, so I spoke up instead.

"How do you plan to move on if you can't even open up to anyone other than your dead husband?"

And as soon as the words left my mouth I wished that I could take them back. She stopped and just stood there for a second then turned around and slowly walked back over to me. I knew I had it coming but somehow it still caught me off guard when she slapped me across the face. I closed my eyes for a second, took a deep breath then exhaled before I opened my eyes and met her gaze. She glared back at me her eyes filling with tears.

"Fuck you, Brendan. I gave you a part of me that I've never shared with anyone else other than my husband and the only thing that I asked from you in return was for us to take it slow." She said her voice a radiating as she spoke.

"I'm sorry," I begin but stopped when she puts her hand up.

"Why would you do that to me, Brendan."

"I only did what you said. You told me you weren't ready, you told me to move on and I did."

She laughs then steps closer to me, "You know what I've been doing since that day?" she asks.

"No," I reply.

"I've been beating myself up because of what I'd said to you. Making appointments with my therapist just so that I can learn how to open up more and let someone else in, I was doing that all for you. But what did you do? You did exactly what every other man on earth does when they don't get what they want when they want it, you went out and found a replacement."

I stood there silent looking her in the eyes not knowing what to say back to her because she was absolutely right, and I was wrong. And maybe it's because my feelings for her weren't what I thought they were, maybe it's because I'm not ready for a relationship either.

"You're right," I begin, "Marissa I do have feelings for you and I honestly care about your kids, but if you're not ready to move on from your husband then I have no choice but to walk away. I wasted seven years of my life on a woman that wasn't sure if she should choose me and I can't do that again. So maybe it's best to stop this now and go on with our lives so that no one gets hurt in the end."

I swallow hard and watch her expression as I wait for her to respond and for a second, I thought she was just going to turn away without saying anything. But she wipes the tears away that had fallen and steps towards me and stands on her toes and kisses me on the cheek, holding my gaze for a brief moment before smiling and turning to walk away.

She hadn't said anything but somehow her unspoken words were loud and clear, and I was sure at that very moment that things between us were over. There would be no hard feelings and if we were to ever cross paths again there would be nothing but a respectable friendship between the two of us. I walked back to the bar and saw that Chasity was standing outside waiting for me and I let out a long breath before I got over to her. I watched as Marissa walked into the embrace that was waiting for her from her sister and friend before turning my focus back to Chasity.

"So, you and my aunt's friend, huh?" She said looking down at the ground.

"Yeah. Um, look, I'm sorry about all this I didn't know that the two of you knew each other."

"I know. My aunt filled me in on what was going on." She said with a smile. "Look if you have feelings for her or something I completely understand, no hard feeling."

141

I reach out and pull her into my arms and she wrapped her arms around me returning the embrace. I release her, and she smiles up at me before turning and walking over to join the other ladies and they head off to their car.

I go back inside the bar and take my seat back at the table. They all stop and look at me, but I just pick up my beer and take a drink and they all go back to their conversations. I saw the look on Janice's face and I'm sure that I'll get one of her talks tomorrow morning but for now, it was time to kick it up a notch and order a few shots.

****

Christmas is a week away and I still haven't packed for the trip to my parent's house and I leave tomorrow morning. After the clinic closed I rushed home and started sorting through my things and getting my bags packed. Once I was done I wrapped the last-minute gifts that I'd bought for my brother and a few other family members and bagged them so that I could toss them in the trunk.

I drop my bags by the door just as my phone rings and I look down and see that it's Marissa calling. I didn't know what to think at first because it's been a couple of weeks since that night at the bar and she hasn't spoken to me since but then another thought crossed my mind and I answered just to make sure it wasn't an emergency.

"Hello," I said picking up at the start of the fourth ring, but the line was silent, and I repeated myself.

"Mr. Brendan," a small voice came over the line and I knew it was Josh.

"Hey, buddy, what's going on?" I ask.

"Nothing much," He said so low that I could barely hear him. "Mr. Brendan, can I ask you a question?"

"Sure, of course. You can always talk to me, Josh." I say, and the line goes silent again for a brief moment.

He lets out a heavy sigh and then continues, "My moms been crying a lot lately and—well I was just wondering if you could come over and talk to her? She's always happy whenever you're around and now that you don't come around anymore she's always sad."

My heart drops from my chest and my mouth goes dry as I listen to what her son is telling me. I swallow hard trying to get the lump out of my throat before speaking but it doesn't go away.

"Josh, I-I don't think that your mom wants to see me right now buddy."

"But she does," He says cutting me off, "I heard her telling aunt Nat that she misses you. Jasmine and I do too."

"I miss you all too little man." I tell him, "You know what how about I come and spend new year with you all."

"Really!"

"Yeah but let's kept it a secret for now so that we can surprise your mom, ok."

"OK, I promise. Bye, Mr. Brendan."

"Later, Josh."

He hangs up the phone and I let out a deep sigh. I take my bags out to the car and then come back inside and go up to my room to get ready for bed so that I can get a good rest before my drive to Knoxville in the morning.

I wake up at 7 am and slip on a pair of sweatpants and my college hoodie and head out to the car. I slide into the driver's seat and start the car then press the button for the garage and it slowly opens. I stop and grab some breakfast before getting on the highway, I probably should have stopped for coffee as well, but I guess I'll just have to settle for an energy drink.

The roads weren't as bad as I thought they'd be and there was surprisingly no heavy traffic on the interstate. Which was great because I made good time and arrived in a little under three hours. I pull into the driveway of my parent's house and my father and brother were standing outside by his truck talking so I parked the car and stepped out calling over to them.

"Hey, what's up little bro," Kyle calls out.

"Dude, two minutes bro," I replied shaking my head at him.

"Doesn't make a bit of difference I'm still the oldest."

My father laughs at the both of us and comes over giving me a quick embrace then releases me and we walk back over to Kyle and I hug my brother.

"Glad to see nothing's changed with you two," My father says with a chuckle.

"Yeah, he's still crying about being the youngest." He says looking over at me and I throw up my middle finger at him and he laughs.

144

They both help me get my bags out of the car then we go inside. Everything was pretty much the way I remembered it except for a few changes here and there that my mother had done to the décor. But it was still home and the smell of fried chicken lingering in the air made it seem even more so.

"There are my sweet boys," My mom said rushing over to us and wrapping her arms around each of us and kissing us on the cheeks.

"Hey ma," we said in unison and she giggled.

"Lord, I sure have missed you, boys. You're going to have to come around a little more and one of you need to bring me home some grandbabies."

My brother and I look at each other then back at my mother and she let out a gut-busting laugh at the expression on our faces. Kids were not in my plans well at least not at the moment, but I'm sure someday I'll have a little mini version of me running around now that I'm much more open to having kids. After being around Marissa and her children something in me changed or maybe that's just it, it's because I can see Marissa and myself having a child together.

"Is everything ok sweetie," My mother asks.

"Yeah ma," I say shaking the thoughts of Marissa from my mind and putting a smile on my face.

"Alright, if you say so." She replies with a knowing smile. "Look here come on in this kitchen and help your mother peel these potatoes."

"Yes, ma'am. I'll be right there."

Chapter Sixteen

Marissa

My feelings were hurt when I saw Brendan hugged up with Chasity at the bar and I can't really explain why. I told him that I wasn't ready when I should've told him that I wanted to be with him. I told him to move on and pushed him away when I should've kept him close and continued to take things slow.

I let out a long sigh and pick up my phone and look through the pictures that we'd taken with the kids at the restaurant the night he took us all out. Tears begin to run down my cheeks, but I quickly swipe them away when I notice Josh enter the room. He comes over and climbs into the bed and lays beside me and snuggling up beside me.

"Mom, why are you always crying?" He asks.

"I just miss daddy sweetheart."

"So, do we. But you know what mom, I think dad sent us Brendan. You know so that we're not alone. And so that you could have someone to love again and not feel so sad."

"Is that so?" I say rubbing my fingers through his hair.

"Yes, your always happy and smiling whenever he's around and he's always there for Jasmine and me." He said, "I don't think that dad would want you to be alone forever mom. I think you should give Mr. Brendan a chance."

"I love you," I whisper in his ear and kiss the top of his head. "You and your sister go and get dressed so that you can come to the restaurant with me today."

"Okay!" He shouts and jumps up from the bed with a huge smile on his face.

I smile and wipe away my tears before getting out of the bed. My son was right no more time for tears, it was time to get back to enjoying life and build a future hopefully with Brendan. I loved my husband, and I would give anything to have him back, but I know that's not possible, so it's time to move on.

School is out, and it's been a packed house almost every night at the restaurant. It's also a week before Christmas so everyone is out enjoying themselves and spending time with their families that are visiting for the holidays. We tend to resonate more business during this time of year especially with all the people visiting from out of town and families wanting to dine out before everything closes for Christmas day.

I get some paperwork done before walking the floor, greeting people and checking on my staff. Everything was running smooth and all of my staff is happy which made me happy. The kids and I had eaten dinner at the restaurant before heading home. I'm not really in the mood to cook tonight and it also gave them a chance to be picky for once.

After leaving the restaurant we stopped by the library to grab a few movies and books. Reading to them when they were babies really paid off, I can't get them to keep their heads out of a book long enough to do most anything else. I'm not complaining though I love that they love to read just as much as I do, and I think it gives all three of us a closer connection.

147

When we get home, we get settled in and make the snacks for our movie night before snuggling up in front of the tv for the rest of the night.

****

I turn on the stove and pour the milk into a small pan and wait for it to warm. It's Christmas morning and my parents should be arriving sometime soon along with my sister and her boyfriend. Everyone expects my homemade hot chocolate on Christmas mornings, so I decided to spruce it up a little and add a few things to make it more festive.

By the time the kids had climbed out of bed my parents were ringing the doorbell. I open the door and greet everyone as they enter then help my dad bring in the presents from the car. I was surprised to see my aunt and a few of my cousins from California pull in to the driveway, my mom hadn't mentioned to me that they would be here for Christmas. But I was happy to see them none the less and very excited that the kids and I will have a chance to meet the newest addition to our family. Two of my cousins have had babies in the last two years and last Christmas they didn't make it to see us, so this is a great surprise.

My cousins and my sister help me out in the kitchen as we prepare everyone's mugs of hot chocolate, then head into the living room to join the rest of the family. We watch as all the kids open their gifts and then the adults exchange their gifts right after. I bought my dad a new set of tools, which he loved, and for my mother, my sister and I bought her a gift card for a complete makeover at the local spa that she loves. The kids got tunes of new toys and electronics from their grandparents and gift cards from my aunt and cousins. My parents got my sister and I round trip tickets for two to Bora

Bora with all expenses paid and my sister was over the moon but me not so much. I'm pretty sure that my parents bought the gift with Brendan in mind and I'm sure this would've been the perfect trip for the two of us to spend some time alone and get to know each other more but oh well.

Me and the ladies head into the kitchen to get dinner started while the fellas head into the den to watch the sports channel and have a few beers. The rest of our family will arrive later this afternoon and that's when the fun beginnings.

"So, is uncle jack coming to Christmas dinner this year?" I ask.

"Oh, geez. I sure hope not," Natalie said rolling her eyes at the thought and we all laugh.

"Don't be that towards your uncle, Nat," my mother says looking over at my sister from the corner of her eyes.

"What," Natalie said, "Oh, come on mom. All he does is get wasted then falls asleep on the sofa with his fly undone."

"Well, at least he's quiet. Cousin Gina likes to get wasted and then try and give everyone advice on how to live their lives," my cousin Marie said.

"True," we all say in unison.

Our Christmas dinners are entertaining and there is never a dull moment throughout the whole night. But every family has that one or two crazy family members that keep the holidays enticing.

"Will Brendan be joining us?" My mother says and my sister chokes on her drink and begins coughing loudly getting my mother's attention.

149

She clears her throat then says, "I'm ok," as she looks over at me.

I knew what she was doing, and I was surprised that she tried to take the heat off me. She's usually quick to watch me gravel while my mom grills me and call me out on my love life. My mom hands my sister a glass of water then looks over at me and notices the look on my face.

"Oh, Marissa," She begins, "Don't tell me that you let that hot hunky doctor get away.

"Mom, I really wish you'd stop calling him that." I snap.

"Mm... a doctor that's hot and hunky. I'm intrigued tell me more." My cousin says taking a seat at the island.

"There's nothing to tell," I say and they all look at me with squinted eyes.

"Marissa, you're not still using Chandler as an excuse as to why you're not dating are you?" My cousin Naomi asks.

I stay silent and stare into the bowl of mashed potatoes that I'm stirring. My mother makes a sound in her throat and shakes her head, but I continue to ignore the question.

"Aw, love... we know how much you loved Chandler, but it's been three years sweetheart you've got to move on," says my aunt Jesse.

"I'm trying," I begin, and tears sting my eyes. "I wake up every morning and tell myself that I'm going to do things differently today and not be afraid to put myself out there. But then something that day comes rushing back to me and I start to feel guilty for even thinking of moving on."

"Honey, you have to let all of that go. We all loved him and we both know that he wouldn't want you to spend the rest of your life feeling sad or alone." Aunt Jesse said, before coming over and putting her arm around me.

"It's time to get back out there, sis and allow someone to love you and treat you like a queen," Natalie said with a smile and a wink.

I take a deep breath and exhale before drying my tears. "You all are right, and I promise that I will give the next guy that comes into my life a chance."

"Next guy," Natalie shouts, "Oh, no...honey you need to call up Dr. Handsome and work your shit out."

My mother walks over to Nat and gives her a high five and we all laughs. I give each of them a hug and then we get back to cooking dinner, all the love and support that they've shown makes my heart smile. I'm glad to have such strong women in my life and I'm thankful for there honest even though sometimes it seems a bit harsh, I know they mean well.

I step away from the ladies once everything was prepared and, in the oven, to try and call Brendan. The phone rings a few times and then it goes to voicemail, so I hang up and try calling again but no answer. I thought about leaving him a voicemail and asking him to call me back so that we could talk but I'm sure he's probably spending time with his family.

The rest of our family finally arrives, and we open gifts with them before having dinner. Once we're done eating we start the festive games that we play each year with the kids. My cousin Gina surprised us this year and showed up sober to

Christmas dinner and even brought gifts for everyone. She also announced that she'd completed rehab and has been sober for eight months and we were all happy to hear that. Although I think I'm going to miss all her crazy antics every year during the holidays.

Our family dance competition is the last game of the night and the one thing that I've been anxiously awaiting. The dance competition can get competitive and my mom and dad are usually the ones that leave victories, but tonight the kids and me we're going to be celebrating after we spank them with our choreographed dance routine. After my parents end their dance with a gyrating hip thrusting move that they seem to use every year to end their dance, my cousins each have their turns with each of their families. The kids and I decided to go last since we were the only family to go all out this year and have a choreographed routine complete with props.

The music starts, and the kids and I dance to Megan Trainers 'All about that bass'. Once our routine was over we received a standing ovation from all of our family and then the winners were announced. Jasmine bounced up and down when we were handed the first-place trophy and Josh spun around and gave me a high five.

I was a little hesitant at first about having everyone over to my house for Christmas this year but everything about this day has been perfect and the smiles on my kids faces made it all the more special.

Chapter Seventeen

Brendan

The past couple of days have been great and I've really enjoyed catching up with my father and brother as well as the rest of my family. We woke up this morning and opened our gifts and had breakfast before heading out back to fire up the grill. My family is unlike most other families during the holidays. While others are cooking up big hams and all of the other festive dishes that people eat on Christmas, my parents have always been the type to go the untraditional route and throw a few ribs and steaks on the grill. My mom makes her special side dishes and fried chicken to go along with everything else.

My dad Carl was born in Trinidad and my mom Martha was born and raised right here in Knoxville, Tennessee. My mom is white and was raised in a very strict and religious household, so every Christmas was done up the traditional way. As for my father, his family is not religious, and they didn't do things the way my mother and her family did, and I think that's what she liked most about my father he didn't live by any rules or restrictions.

After having a few beers with my father and my brother I head upstairs to shower and get dressed before the rest of our family shows up. I'd thought about calling Marissa and wishing them a Merry Christmas, but I decided against it. Besides, I'm not sure if she's ready to talk to me or if she really wants to but she's been on my mind heavily ever since I spoke with Josh. I push the thoughts to the back of my mind and finish getting ready then head back downstairs. A few of my family members had arrived and were sitting in the den with my father watching sports center.

"Hey son, come join us. Your grandfather was just asking about you." My father says waving me over.

I walk over and give my grandpa a hug before taking a seat in the reclining chair across from him. "So how are things going with your practice son?" My father asks.

"Everything is great, dad," I reply.

"That's good," he said. "And what about that young lady your brother was telling me about. How are things there?" my dad asks.

I take a deep breath and slowly exhale before answering. "Uh, that's kind of over now dad."

"Well, what did you do?" ask my grandad. "You're not still fawning over that fast-tailed woman that left you, now are you?"

"No, grandpa," I chuckle.

"Well, then what is boy?"

"Marissa lost her husband a few years ago and she's just not ready to let go," I answer.

"Oh, now I see. You got you one of those damaged women," said my grandpa.

"Dad," my father shouts but my grandpa ignores him.

"Does she have any kids?" grandpa asks.

"Yes, she has two," I say.

"Oh, well hell you don't want to do that then son." My grandpa said scooting to the edge of his seat.

My grandpa is old and very outspoken but that didn't come with the old age either. He's always been the one to tell us like it is and he doesn't hold back when he lands his punches. But it made my brother and me strong, and it made us both assholes, but hey we get it honest.

The house starts to fill with a lot more of our family members and close family friends. The quiet and relaxed atmosphere was now gone. Music was playing in one room, people talking in another, and the kitchen was filled with the sound of pots, pans, and laughter. My mother and several other women in the family were talking and cooking while having a glass of wine in the kitchen. There are kids everywhere, running from room to room, screaming, and chasing one another. I go out to the guest house to try and have a moment of silence. But when I push open the front door I see my brother with his back against the wall and his pants down around his ankles. I look down at the petite woman down on her knees with my brother's dick in her mouth and my mouth drops.

"Well, well I was wondering where you'd been all day bro," I say, and his eyes shoot open and the gorgeous woman in front of him slowly stands to her feet with a smile on her face.

"What the fuck Brendan get out," He shouts pulling up his pants.

"I didn't know you had a twin Kyle," she said staring at me and biting her bottom lip. "I've never had twins before can he join us," she asks.

My brother's eyes get wide and he looks over at her and then over at me and I couldn't help but laugh. I could tell that she was the type of girl that you only take home for the night, but my brother, he thinks that every pretty girl is sweet and innocent.

"I think you should probably go now," Kyle says.

"Ok," she shrugs her shoulders and begins walking away. "If you boys change your mind, Kyle, you know how to reach me."

I watch her as she walks past me and out the door and closing it behind her. I look over at my brother watching as he walks over to the large red sofa and falls back onto it letting out a long sigh. I shake my head and go over to join him kicking off my shoes and putting my feet up on the ottoman.

"So where did you meet this one?" I ask.

"The mall," he replies in a low voice.

I bust out laughing and he picks up one of the pillows from the sofa and tosses it at me and making a low growling noise. I catch the pillow and throw it back at him, but he swipes it with his hand before it hits him.

"You've got to stop bringing home these women you meet at the mall," I say.

"But she seemed so sweet," he replies.

"Yeah, I know. Those are the ones that are usually the closet freaks." I say smirking at him.

"Oh my gosh," he shouts, "Why can't I for once find a nice decent girl." He screams out and throws his hands in the air.

"There are plenty of them, bro," I say.

"Yeah I guess so I mean you found one so maybe there's hope for me yet." He laughs and tosses the pillow in the air.

He was right I had found a great woman with two amazing kids that I was starting care for deeply. How do I manage to fuck up everything with the first good woman that's come into my life? Instead of rushing her to make a decision on whether or not we were going to be together I should have just gone with the flow and took things as slow as she wanted, and we'd still be together. Because the truth is I've already fallen in love with her and if she needs me to wait a decade I'm ready and willing to do whatever it takes.

We sit and talk a little longer and I invite him to come visit me in Nashville so that we can hang out and I can hook him up with a few potential girlfriends. My dad comes out and lets us know that it's time for dinner, and we all head back inside to join the rest of the family. We all gather around the table and say grace then everyone digs in piling there plates full and we all converse while we eat catching up with one another and listening to everyone's stories about what's happening in their lives.

After dinner, everyone settled into their own spaces and I headed up to my room. It's been a long day, but I enjoyed catching up with all of my family especially my parents, my brother, and my grandparents. I'm going to have to start making a much better effort to get home and spend Christmas with my family each year. I go into my room and fall across the bed and let out a sigh of relief as I pull one of the pillows under my head. I roll over and grab my phone from the bedside table and press the unlock button and the screen lights up. I sit up straight on the bed and stare down at the

157

screen at the two missed calls from Marissa that appeared, and my heart jumps into my throat. She'd called me earlier while I was having dinner with my family and I missed it I look over at the clock and see that it's kind of late, so I decide not to call back.

I lie back on the bed and put the pillow back under my head with a wide toothy smile on my face. I was glad to know that she was thinking about me just as much as I was thinking about her. Who knows maybe next Christmas we'd spend it together and end our night in each other's arms, or with her legs touching the headboard while she screams my name, either way, is fine with me.

****

I pull into my parking space and grab my things from the back seat and head inside. I say hello to the patients that are sitting in the waiting area and then my staff as I head back to my office. I hang my coat and then set my bag on the couch before walking over and taking a seat behind my desk.

"Welcome back doctor," Janice says as she steps into my office.

"Good morning Janice," I say smiling at her.

"How did the visit go with your family?" she asks.

"It was great. I plan to try and make it home every year I really enjoyed spending time with my parents."

"That's awesome. Well, I hope you're well rested and ready to work because it seems like the flu is making its rounds." She said dropping the folders on to my desk and heading out the door.

Our schedules are booked up today for appointments and sick visits. It was so chaotic today that I really couldn't tell if I was coming or going and when I finally had the chance to take a quick break I locked myself in my office. I laid back on the couch and shut my eyes trying to relax and calm the pounding headache that was taking over my brain. My phone buzzed in my coat pocket and I reached in and pulled it and pressed the button without checking to see who was calling.

"Yeah," I said into the phone.

"Hi, Brendan," Marissa said in a low voice and my eyes shot open.

"Hey," I reply.

"Um...did I call at a bad time? I can call back if you're busy?" she said.

"No, no it's fine. I'm actually sitting in my office taking a quick break."

"Oh, ok. Well, I was just calling to see if you could stop by the restaurant later?"

"Sure, I'll stop by once I leave the office."

"Ok, I'll see soon," she says then ends the call.

I press the button and lock my phone before sliding it back into my jacket pocket. I go over to my desk and take a bottle of painkillers from my drawer and grab a bottle of water from the mini fridge sitting in the corner of my office. It seemed as though the rest of the day had breezed by after I'd spoken with Marissa or maybe it was just because I was anxious to meet up with her. I miss her and the kids and

159

hopefully tonight everything will go back to the way it was, and we can move towards the future together.

After I finish up with my last patient I head into my office and close the door so that I could change into the pair of jeans and t-shirt that I keep in my office. I say goodnight to my staff and colleagues then head out to my car. I pull up to the curb and park the car and go inside where I'm greeted and then taken to a table in the back of the restaurant were Marissa told them to seat me once I'd arrived. The waitress came over to take my food and drink order then disappeared to go and put it in. The young waitress returned a few minutes later and placed my drink on the table and let me know that my food would be out momentarily. I thanked her, and she disappeared once again, ten minutes later Marissa came walking up to the table with our food in hand. She sat the plates on the table and I stood to hug her, and she leaned into me returning the gentle embrace.

"I missed you," I said, the words pouring out of my mouth before I could catch myself.

She pulls back and looks into my eyes, "I missed you too Brendan," she replied a small smile on her lips.

I kiss her on her forehead then release her and we both take our seats next to each other. She looks beautiful and the way that her dress is hugging her hips makes me want to do all kinds of nasty things to her right here, right now. I focus on the plate in front of me as we begin eating our meal because all that I can really think about is how I would prefer to have my hands and mouth all over her.

"So, how is everything with you?" She asks.

"It's great. I got to spend some time with my parents and my twin brother for the holidays."

"There's two of you?" She asks shocked.

"Yeah, there is," I chuckle.

"Oh...." She said her eyes wide, "Is he just as charming and um—handsome as you are?"

"I guess you could say that I mean we are identical," I reply.

"Is he single?" she asks with a smirk.

"Maybe... Are you looking?" I ask with a raised brow.

"No. I've already fallen in love—," she beings to say then stops mid-sentence.

I look over at her and she turns away from me looking down at her plate, her cheeks are a light shade of red and a smile on her face. A part of me knows what she's going to say but I still want to hear her say the words. I wait a few seconds before saying anything just to see if she's going to finish the rest of her sentence. But she doesn't, she remains silent, picks her fork up from her plate, and continues eating.

"Do you have any plans for New Year's Eve?" I asked breaking the silence.

"No. I usually hang out with my Nat, Belia, and Trista. But this year Nat's spending it with her boyfriend and Belia and Trista have plans. It's ok though I think I'd rather spend it with the kids anyways." She replies.

Great, she's going to be home alone with the kids so my plan to surprise her will be able to go off without a hitch. I'm glad that she didn't make any plans because it would've made it

161

harder to crash her get together with her friends and their unpredictable night out.

"What about you? Do you have any plans to bring in the New Year?" She asks.

"uh, yeah I have a little something planned," I reply before taking a sip of my drink watching the expression on her face.

I could see the hint of disappointment that was on her face and I'm sure it's because she's probably thinking that I have plans with another woman. And I would tell her otherwise, but I don't want to say too much and ruin the surprise or give her any hints about my plan to spend the night making love to her in every position imaginable. After we finish our main course we order dessert and talk more while we wait for it to be brought out.

"Brendan, the reason that I ask you to meet me here tonight is that I wanted to apologize for the way that I've been stringing you along."

"I think we both—,"

"Please, let me finish so I don't lose my nerve." She says cutting me off and I motion for her to continue.

"After Chandler passed away it was like my world ended. The kids and I were so devastated, and I told myself that I would never allow another man to come into our lives and take his place. I was going to remain single and live my life alone and for two and a half years I did. But then you came along, and everything felt right again. I feel comfortable and safe with you, you make me laugh, you make me blush, and you make me feel beautiful. I feel alive again and I never

162

thought that it could be possible to feel this way with anyone other than my husband, but I was wrong."

She looks up and her eyes meet my gaze. I couldn't believe how open, honest, and vulnerable she was being. I knew that I couldn't allow her to be the only one to pour out her honest emotions and I not do the same. Because the truth is that we're both damaged and we're both trying to move past a devastating situation in each of our lives. I need to let her know that she's not alone and that we can both move past it even if it's not together.

"Listen, Marissa, I understand what you're saying, and I want you to know that you're not alone because I've been holding back as well. When Nia left me, I was heartbroken, and I vowed to never trust another woman or to put that much time or energy into another relationship and have it fail. But when I met you I knew that there was something different about you, you made me feel things that I never wanted to allow myself to feel again."

She glances over at me with a warm smile on her face then leans in and kisses me. Her lips are so soft, and I could taste the strawberry from her dessert still on her lips. I wrap my arm around her waist and pull her chair in closer to me so that I could pull her into my lap. I'm happy that she had her staff set our table away from the rest of the people that are dining because there was nothing innocent about the kiss we were having. The waitress walks over to our table and she pulls back from our kiss feeling breathy and winded and quickly scoots back over to her seat. The young lady's cheeks turn a bright shade of pink and she apologizes as she removes our dishes from the table. Once she walks away we look over at each other and laugh.

"Omgosh..." She says covering her face. "I don't know what came over me. I'm sorry for jumping you like that I can't believe I just did that." She said with a small laugh.

"It's ok. I think the emotions started to run a little high for a moment there," I replied placing my hand on her back gently rubbing it.

"I think I should probably get back and check on things," she says.

"Ok," I reply, and I stand to my feet and help her from hers. "I hope to see you again soon."

"Me too," She said kissing my cheek as we embrace.

I release her and watch as she walks towards the kitchen and disappears through the doors. I head towards the front of the restaurant and step outside to a cold night air hitting me in the face. I tug my coat together and pull my hood onto my head and walk to my car and climb inside, slowly pulling away from the curb and into the evening traffic.

I walk into the house and hang my coat, I head up to my bedroom and pull off my clothes as I walk into the closet and toss them in the hamper. I turn on the shower and step inside letting the water run over me warming my body. I close my eyes and think about the kiss that Marissa and I shared back at the restaurant and my manhood twitches at the thought. I could get myself off, but I'd much rather be inside of Marissa and in a few days, I will be so I'm going to hold off until then.

Chapter Eighteen

Marissa

I don't know how Brendan seems to always make me feel so relaxed and at ease to the point where I let my guard down and just leap, but he does. I know it must have been quite embarrassing for Mia to walk in on her boss making out. I will have to make sure to apologize to her later after we've closed. I'm shocked that I was brave enough to even do that type of thing and so close to the customers I mean anyone could have seen us. That kiss! It was all that I could think of for the rest of the evening. I'd tried to finish up the paperwork on my desk, but I just simply could not concentrate.

After the crowd died down and my staff worked to close up the restaurant, I tucked away the stack of papers into my draw to finish up tomorrow. I wonder what it is that he'll be doing on New Year's Eve maybe he's going to go back and visit with his family. Maybe he has someone that he's made plans with that evening, no, there is no way he's entertaining anyone else not from the way he kissed me. I push the thoughts to the back of my mind and go out to the front to check on things and see if any of my team needs any help.

"Oh…um, Ms. Wilmore," Mia calls out to me, "I just want to apologize for earlier I didn't mean to interrupt—"

"No, no, it's fine Mia. I actually wanted to apologize to you." I say stopping her.

She giggles. "No need to apologize to me Ms. Wilmore."

"I just wanted to make sure you weren't uncomfortable."

"No way it's totally fine," she says waving it off. "Besides it's nice to see you happy and smiling again. Oh…and he's hot, I sure wouldn't hold back on the PDA either." She winks at me then smiles and turns to walk away.

I was relieved that she wasn't freaked out and she was so right Brendan is hot panty soaking kind of hot. You know what I'm not going to let this go on any longer I know what I want and I'm damn sure going to go for it. I'm going to call Brendan and tell him that it's time for us to stop playing this little game. If I don't snatch him up, then some other woman will and offer him her heart and then it'll be to late for me. I lock up the restaurant and my staff and I walk out to our cars and say a quick goodnight before leaving.

When I get home, I have dinner with the kids and get them into bed then head up to my room and shower. I wash my hair and blow it out before slipping on my pjs and climbing into bed and getting comfortable. I take out my notebook from the drawer on my nightstand and make a shopping list of the items I'll need for my night in with the kids. After I finish I set the notepad and pen on my nightstand and slide down into the bed and roll over onto my side shutting my eyes and falling asleep.

****

I can't believe the year has come to an end so quickly. I can't really say that it was the greatest when it first began but it has turned out to be one hell of an ending. I never in my wildest dreams imagined myself with a man like Brendan, but I'm sure happy that we met and hit off. Boy did we hit it off, like out of the park. He's handsome, he's a doctor, and the sex, oh the sex is so freaking steamy and hot.

166

"Mom can we go now I'm cold?" Jasmine asks tugging at my coat tearing me away from my thoughts.

"Sure princess. Are you sure you don't want to stay a little longer with your friends?" I reply, and she shakes her head quickly from side to side saying no. "Alright well let's get your jacket then tell your friends goodbye, ok?"

"Ok," she says.

Some of the parents from Jasmines school invited her to ice skate with their children. She was content for about an hour or so but quickly lost interest after falling a few times. The other girls tried to help her out, but she wasn't feeling up to it after her last flop on the ice. She told me it was cold and that her tush was getting really cold after that, so I knew it wouldn't be long before she'd ask to leave. We say goodbye to everyone and then head out to the car. She bounces inside and buckles her seat belt and then I join her, starting the car and backing out of the parking space.

I drop Jasmine off with my mom and wave bye as I pull away from the house. Josh is out with my father for the evening having a little guy time and Jasmine wanted to spend time with her grandmother. I drive over to the restaurant and check up on my staff then stop by the shopping mall to grab a few things before heading home. I pull into the driveway and notice my sister sitting in her car waiting for me.

"Hey sis," she says as I step out of the car.

"What's up Nat?" I ask.

"Nothing much. Just thought I'd drop by and visit the best sister in the world." She replies.

167

I stop and gaze at her my eyes hooded, "Ok, what did you do? And will it cost me money?" I ask.

"No," she says laughing historically and waving her hand at me.

"Oh, shit Nat don't tell me your pregnant?" I say panicked.

"Omgosh…No, would you stop." She says opening the car door and grabbing the bags from the seat on her side.

"Well what is it? I know you didn't just drop by for a pow wow,"

She follows me into the house and places the bags on the kitchen counter then turns and jumps up onto it taking a seat. She pulls an apple from the bag and bites into it all the while watching me as I move around the kitchen putting away the things from the bags. I couldn't take her agonizing silence, so I stop what I'm doing and lean against the counter with my arms folded across my chest.

"What?" She asks.

"Ok… spill it. What are you doing here?"

She sucks in a deep breath and hangs her head, "I just wanted to get away for a while."

I huff, "Oh my gosh here we go again." I say pushing myself from the counter.

"Marissa,"

"No, Nat you always do this every time you start to get close to a guy or you begin to have feelings for him."

"I do not,"

"Yes. You. Do!" I say spinning back around to face her. "This guy is actually good for you Nat. Why do you want to ruin a good thing?"

She rolls her eyes and hops down off the counter and throws the half-eaten apple into the trash and comes over and gives me a hug. "I think I'm going to go, nice talking to you sis."

"Natalie, are you really going to just walk away."

"I'll call you later sis."

"Natalie!" I call out to her, but she just keeps walking and a couple of seconds later the door opens and closes.

I take a deep breath and let out a long sigh. I hate when she does that, just walks away in the middle of our conversations. I don't understand why she is so stubborn or why she insists on bottling her feelings up and never letting anyone in. Ever since the last serious relationship that she was in, right before she left for college ended with her high school sweetheart. She's been closed off and distant from every man she's ever met or that she gets close to. I don't know maybe she's still holding on to that break up or hoping that it'll one day come back around but I do know that she's never going to get past it if she doesn't talk about it with someone.

I make myself a cup of tea and head into the living room and get comfortable on the sofa with my latest romance novel and begin to read. The sound of the doorbell startles me awake, I'd fallen asleep while reading. The sun had gone down, and night began to fall as the street lights flickered to life. I get up from the sofa and go to answer the door, I could see a flashlight shining through the glass on the sides of the door. I open the door and find an older gentleman, a police officer, standing in my doorway and my heart leaped into my chest.

169

"Can I help you officer?" I ask.

"Hello ma'am, I'm looking for a Mrs. Wilmore?"

"Yes, that's me. What's going on did something happen?"

He breathes in deep and says, "Um…Ma'am I think you should come with me." the officer responds after a couple of seconds.

"Why?" I ask with an unnerved feeling in my stomach, "Did something happen with my kids or my parents?"

"No ma'am," He says quickly. "There's a problem at your restaurant ma'am, please just come with me and I'll explain on the way."

"What, Omgosh ok give me one second."

I hurry into the mudroom and grab my shoes then my purse and keys from the table in the foyer and rush out the door following the officer. As we neared the restaurant the panic grew stronger as I noticed all of the flashing lights, police cars, and fire trucks positioned outside. The officer slows to a stop and I open the door and jump out of the car jogging over to where my assistant manager was standing talking to the fire chief.

"Thank god, Marissa. I don't know what happened they say the restaurant caught fire a couple hours ago, but no one is sure how." She says he voice shaky.

"Mrs. Wilmore," the chief says, "Were there any bad wiring or hazards that you know of that could've started the fire?"

"No, I mean everything is new and up to date. We just had an inspection not to long ago and everything was up to code." I say placing my hand over my mouth as I look onto the site.

"Well were going to look into it once we get the fire out and everything under control and then we'll let you know what we find." He says, and I shake my head because I was at a loss for words. He pats my shoulder then turns and walks over to the officer that was waiting for him.

I couldn't believe it all of my hard work and time spent building this place into a success has gone up in flames. How am I going to come back from this, I know that the insurance will cover all of the damages and it'll be more than enough to rebuild. But still all of the memories I've shared with Chandler and the kids have been erased. Tears sting my eye then force there way out and stream down my cheeks as a low sob escapes me.

"Oh no, Ms. Wilmore, everything will be alright." Karen says wrapping her arms loosely around my shoulders comforting me. "Is there anyone that you want for me to call for you? Or anything that you need for me to do?"

"No, I'm ok." I reply wiping my tears with the back of my coat sleeve. "You can head home, I'll call you later and give you an update."

"Ok, please call me if there's anything, anything at all."

"I will. Thanks Karen." She blows me a kiss then heads off to her car.

I take out my phone and send a message to Brendan telling him what happened. I call my parents and let them know what was going on and ask if they could keep the kids a couple of days while I sort things out. My heart is shattered, I don't understand what could've gone wrong. I'm very careful, I quickly repair things that need to be fixed, I've replaced all of the old wiring, and the appliances.

171

I take a deep breath and exhale gathering myself before going back over to speak with the officer and the fire chief. I hear someone call my name and I turn to see who it is, Brendan was climbing out of his SUV just as I turn and look in his direction. He shuts the door and rushes over to me pulling me into his arms.

"What the hell happened?" He says kissing the top of my head. "Are you ok? Did anyone get hurt?" He asks panicked.

"Everyone is fine. None of my staff were inside, the restaurant was closed for the day." I reply wrapping my arms around his waist and holding him tight.

"Thank goodness. You scared the shit out of me." He said pulling back and gazing into my eyes.

"I'm sorry," I say in a soft voice that is almost a whisper.

"Do they know what happened?"

"No, they're still trying to get all of the fire out." I say pushing my face into his chest. "Thank you so much for coming Brendan."

"Of course, Marissa I'll be here anytime you need me to be." He says.

"I know…but still thank you." I reply.

He stays by my side the whole time until the officer told us that we should get out of there and go home and get some rest. After he drove me home and I thought that he was only going to walk me to the door and wish me a goodnight, but he joined me inside. I sat on the couch while he made me a hot cup of tea to help calm me a little. He returns and sits the drinks on the table and sits beside me on the sofa pulling me into him. I slide over and snuggle in close resting my head on his shoulder and tears begin rolling down once again.

"I'm sorry that this happened to you, Marissa." He said, "But you're a strong woman and you'll figure out a way to bounce back from all this."

"Yeah…it's just that," I begin but I pause.

"What is it?" He asks.

"I feel like I'm losing everything in my life that matters to me, everything that I love."

"The memories that you and your husband have made there will still be there because you carry them with you. The only thing that's going to change is the building structure."

I take a second to let all the he's saying sink in and then I sit up on the sofa and I dry my tears. He was right the building is just that but the memories and all of the things that I cherish most are in my children and me. and it's not like I can't rebuild it just that this time I'll be doing it alone. And once again the sadness I was feeling before creeps back up on me now that I realize that I'm alone.

"If you want I can help you with the rebuild and anything else that you may need." He said, and I swear it's like he can read my thoughts.

"I couldn't ask you to do that," I reply.

"Well it's a good thing you're not asking," he said the corner of his lips turning up into a small smile.

I throw my arms around him and let out a laugh as he falls back onto the couch. I missed him so much and his witty sarcasm as well, I wish that we could just put everything behind us and move towards the future. He's been so compassionate and understanding of me and all of my issues and gosh he loves my kids and all of the chaos that comes along with them. I never thought that it would be possible to find a man that would accept us the way he has because let's face it most guys are douches. But he's really proving himself to not only me but to my kids and our lives as well.

Now if only he'd give me another chance!

Chapter Nineteen

Brendan

I knew after everything that had happened tonight with her restaurant was a blow to the chest and I felt for Marissa. Losing something that you've built and grown into something successful hits hard once it's taken from you. I wanted to be here to comfort her and let her know that she's not alone in any of this and to assure her that I will help her in any way that I can. After a few tears and a couple of glasses of wine she's finally fallen asleep and I carried her up to her room and got her into bed. I cuddle up beside her and laid beside her until I drifted off to sleep, it felt so good to be next to her.

The next morning a faint giggle wakes me, and I open my eyes as I roll over onto my back. For a moment I thought that maybe I was dreaming, and the noise wasn't real then I heard it again. I shift myself in the bed and sit up on my elbows and look around the room, leaning at the end of the bed was the cutest little pigtailed girl I've ever seen in my life staring at me with a wide grin on her face.

"Good Morning Mr. Brendan," she says wiggling from side to side with her hands folded together under her chin.

"Good Morning to you Princess Jasmine," I reply and sit up in the bed.

She giggles again and hops onto the bed crawling her way up to me and bouncing on to my lap putting her arms around my neck and hugging me tightly. What is this feeling? I've never

175

felt this kind of flutter in my heart before not for anyone. The warmth and the joy that fills my heart every time I'm near this sweet little girl. Every part of me wants to love her and protect her from all of the dangers of the world and teach her about life.

"Mr. Brendan you have really big arms," she says squeezing my biceps pulling me from my thoughts.

"I don't think they're that big," I reply.

"Seriously, these things are massive," she says and for the first time, I notice that she has the cutest little lisp.

I chuckle and lift her up with one quick swoop pulling her into the air. "Well you see they have to be big and strong so that I can help you to fly high," I say getting up from the bed and flying her around the room.

"Woo... yay! Higher, higher," she shouts.

Marissa wakes up and rolls over on to her side and her eyes lock on us. She has the most beautiful smile appear on her face as she watches the two of us play around. She sits up in the bed rests her back against the headboard and laughs at the two of us.

"Mommy, Mommy, look I'm flying," She calls out.

"I see. I hope you haven't eaten breakfast yet," Marissa says looking at me with a smirk on her face.

"I had waffles," she says stretching her arms out to her side like wings on a plane.

I look over at Marissa and she gives me a look and I stop spinning and place Jasmine back onto her feet. I keep my hand on her arms for a second so that she doesn't fall over, she wobbles a few times and then she finally balances herself and looks up at me and smiles.

"That was fun I wanna do it again," she says reaching her arms up to me.

"Um, how about we let your food digest and then we'll give it another go, ok?"

She's silent for a second then says, "Ok," then runs out of the room and heads downstairs.

I shake my head and walk back over to the bed and slide in beside her pulling her face to mine. She closes her eyes and leans into the kiss, I don't think that I'll ever get tired of kissing her soft, full lips. I place my hand on the nape of her neck and pull her in deeper kissing her slow.

"Eww…" we hear a voice say from the doorway.

We break away from each other and look over to the door and see Josh standing there with his hands over his eyes.

"It's safe to look," I say with a chuckle.

"You really are here," He says walking into the room and over to my side of the bed and giving me a hug.

"I am," I reply returning the embrace.

"Sweetheart is your grandmother downstairs?" Marissa asks.

"Yes, ma'am," he replies.

"Ok, give me and Brendan a few minutes and we'll be down,"

"Ok, mom." He runs out the door and closes it behind him.

177

Once the door closed she shifts in the bed and pulls me into another kiss pressing her lips to mine. I feel the need for me and I wanted to give her what she wanted but I just felt like the timing isn't right. I slowly pull away from the kiss and her eyes shoot open.

"What's wrong? Do you want me to lock the door?"

"No," I say.

"I promise I'll be really quiet—or sort of quiet," she giggles then leans in again, but I stop her.

"I think we should wait,"

"Wait? Brendan, I don't want to wait, I want you now,"

"Marissa," I say in a low voice.

She scoots back up into the bed and leans against the headboard once again pulling her legs into her chest. I drop my head and take a breath and slowly exhale before bringing my eyes back up to meet her gaze. I could see that she was thrown off and confused by my rejection, but I don't want to move things along to fast and end up back where we were before.

"Are you not interested in me anymore?" she asks turning away from me like she was afraid of what my answer might be.

I reach over and turn her face back towards me, "That's not it. I just want you to be sure, I want the both of us to be sure, and to be ready."

"But I am—" She begins but I cut her off.

"I love you, Marissa. I want to be with you and I want to be a part of you and your kid's lives, but I need to know that you're ready for all of that as well. I want this to be about more than just sex between the two of us."

She sits quietly for a moment thinking over what I'd said to her then she finally turns to me looking into my eyes. She smiles and places her hand on my cheek as tears begin to fill her eyes and she leans in and kisses me.

"I love you too, Brendan." She whispers. "I promise, I'm ready."

I pull her into my arms and hug her tight as she wraps her arms around me returning the embrace. I never thought I'd feel this way about anyone ever again but everything with Marissa and her kids feels right. I feel like I'm where I belong like this is where I'm meant to be and with whom I was meant to be with.

****

Marissa and the kids have been spending a lot of time at my place and the reconstruction for the restaurant is going well. I must say having them in my home has really brought it back to life, it's doesn't feel so big and cold anymore. It finally has that at home feel once again and it finally looks lived in for once. Although I never knew that two children running through the house could sound like ten and some days I swear it looks like a tsunami ransacked the place. But it's all good I wouldn't change it for the world.

I've been trying to find the time to ask her and the kids to move in with me, but no time ever seems like the right time. I took her and the kids to meet my parents on New Year's Day and after my mother finally got through sobbing and being

179

ecstatic at the thought of grandkids she and Marissa spent some time together and they really hit it off. Actually, she hit it off with my whole family and I think she's kind of sweet on them as well. My brother is happy that I've decided to settle down and the kids they took to him just as quickly, he's already Uncle Kyle. Jasmine's facial expression was priceless when she saw Kyle walking in the door, "Omgosh there's two of you, awesome!" she shouted. Needless to say, for about an hour she got the two of us mixed up but by the end of the night she'd figured out a way to tell us apart.

My days at the office seem to feel longer now that I have a reason to rush home at the end of the day. Hanging out at the bar after work has become a thing of the past well with the acceptation of going for a drink every now and again with my staff.

"Hey Brendan," Jamieson says knocking on the door. "You got a minute?" He asks.

"Sure, come in,"

"I just wanted to see if you were up for a double date on Saturday night?"

"I'll have to run it by Marissa but I'm sure it won't be a problem."

"Great, just keep me posted,"

"Sure thing, I'll shoot you a text later tonight."

He taps the door twice then nods and heads out of the office with a smile on his face. Seems like things are going well between him and his lady plus I'm happy to see him in a more positive mood. I didn't think that he was going to make it for a while there, but things are looking up for him. He's finally gotten his divorce and they came to an agreement and are now sharing custody of their daughter. I pick up my cell and send Marissa a quick text about going out Saturday night she quickly responds with a yes. She's been so focused and stressed out about the restaurant I'm sure she would have agreed to anything that would give her a break from work and the kids for an evening.

"Knock, knock," Janice says as she walks in. "Here are a few papers that need your signature asap and a reminder for the fundraiser next week at the children's hospital."

"Shit, I forgot all about that,"

"I knew you had that's why I took the liberty of putting it on your calendar and a reminder on all of your devices."

"Thanks Janice," I said offering her a smile. "What would I do without you?"

"Let's hope you never have to find out," She winks at me then disappears out the door.

I honestly don't know what I would do without her here she's kept everything going and running smoothly for me. One thing I do know is that she needs a vacation, I've noticed how overwhelmed she's been and I know she always refuses to take one but this time I'm not taking no for an answer. I send an email to my travel agent and have him book a vacation for two to Key West, Florida. A week at the beach lounging around with her husband should do the trick, she can return well rested and ready to get back to it.

I arrive at home a little later than I'd expected to with two last minute patients calling in needing to be seen. I go inside and put my things away before heading into the kitchen, music was playing, and I could smell the food lingering in the air. I stop at the door with a surprised look on my face when I notice Marissa standing by the stove with nothing but an apron covering the front her body.

"Hey baby, you're late," she says with a sexy grin on her face."

"Yeah…I had two last minute calls,"

"Mm, well lucky for you I kept dinner warm and dessert is ready as well."

I chuckle and walk over to her and take the plate from her and set them on the counter and pull her up into my arms. She wraps her legs around my waist as I carry her over to the table pushing the dishes out of the way before laying her on the table. She looks up at me as I untie the apron and pull it over her head, her full breast now on display as she sits before me completely naked. She reaches for my jeans, but I move her hand away and lie her back on the table slowly kissing her from her cheek all the way down to her breast. I take her nipple into my mouth and nibble on it gently as she moans softly running her hands through my hair. I let my hand move down her body slowly to her sex then begin massaging her clit as she slowly began to move sway her hips.

I could feel her juices spilling out onto my fingers, she was ready for me, so warm and so wet. I slide two of my fingers inside of her and her breath catches as I push deeper. I work her g-spot with my fingers until I feel her orgasm getting close, I remove my fingers and position myself in between her legs and take a seat in the chair. I pull her to the end of the table so that the only thing supporting her now is my shoulders. I take my time teasing her sweet spot with my tongue licking, sucking, and devouring her pussy until she couldn't take it anymore.

"Ah...fuck I'm coming," she screams in a high-pitched voice.

Her hips rocked forward thrusting into my face as she gripped a fist full of my hair in her hand as she climaxes, letting her juices fill my mouth. My dick was throbbing it was so fucking hard pressing against my zipper, I stood to my feet and unfastened my jeans letting my erection spring free. I step out of my jeans and pull off my shirt leaving them in a pile on the floor beside the table. She looked so sexy laying there all flushed and breathy waiting for me to finish pleasing her. I lean in and press my lips to hers kissing her slow and passionately as she wrapped herself around me.

"I love you, baby," she whispers.

"I love you more," I replied kissing her hard.

She pushes her hand between us taking my dick into her hand positioning it at her opening, rubbing it across her wetness and I let out a low groan. Will I ever get enough of this woman or will she end up driving me crazy?

"Brendan, please," she whimpers, and I give in and ease slowly inside of her. "Yes..." she moans.

I plunge into her deeper and faster as I feel her tighten around me and her pussy begins to pulse as she reaches another orgasm. She screams out my name and it's the best sound in the world, if only I could I would make her say my name in this octave every day all day for the rest of our lives.

"Fuck," I grunt as I get closer to the edge.

"Yes, Brendan. I want to feel you inside of me baby." She moans loudly and that it's I erupt.

My muscles tense as the pressure builds as my dick spasms inside of her, my body jerks as I pump out each and every moment of our climax. My head is swimming and my body feels weak, so I slowly remove myself and take a seat in the chair by the table. Marissa and I smile at each other as we try and catch our breath, after several minutes she finally slides down from the table and comes over and sits on my lap.

"So, should we eat dinner now that you've had your dessert?" She asks with a smirk on her face.

"I think perhaps we should, you're going to need your strength for what I have in mind for you later."

"Mm..." she moans with a playful giggle.

We fall deeper into the kiss then a buzz from the front gate interrupts us.

"No, don't," I beg, wrapping my arms tighter around her. "Whoever it is they'll go away," I say but she wiggles from my grasp.

"Let's make sure it's nothing important and if it's not I'll send them away," she winks at me then turns and walks into the hallway towards the front entrance.

"Walk slower I'm trying to enjoy the view," I call out to her and she stops for a second and looks back over her shoulder and smacks her ass then continues walking. Leaving me to watch her ass jiggle and shake as she walks away.

She's so fucking sexy and she's all mine.

I slip on my jeans and go over to the stove to grab the food out of the oven. I'd worked up an appetite and I was starving; my lunch today was very light a couple of bites out of my turkey sandwich was all I managed to get in before I was getting called for my next appointment. I cleaned the table and placed all of the settings back in place before fixing our plates.

Marissa walks into the kitchen clearing her throat, "Brendan," she says softly, and I turn to look at her and my heart drops, my body immediately goes numb.

Why the fuck does this woman still have this kind of control over my emotions and why the fuck is she here. I thought we'd gotten closer, I thought that things were over, and I would never have to see again after that day that she showed up with her husband to his appointment. I stood there frozen in place I didn't know what to say to her and from the look on Marissa's face, she could see the effect that she had on me.

"I'm going to let the two of you talk," Marissa says.

"That's not necessary. I'm sure whatever it is that Nia has to say she can say it with you here,"

I watch has Nia's expression changes and her eye lower to the floor. She takes a deep breath and brings her gaze back to mine and clears her throat before speaking.

"I'm sorry to intrude I wasn't aware that you were living with someone," she replies. "Um…I think I should go I'm very sorry for interrupting." She turns and begins to walk away.

"Hey, no," Marissa says stopping her. "Brendan I'm going to go up to our bedroom and wait for you. I think the two of you need to talk."

"Marissa, I don't—" I began, and she holds up her hand to stop me as she takes Nia's arm into hers and walks her over to the table.

"It's ok," she says looking into my eyes. "talk to her, please."

She lifts herself on to her tippy toes and gives me a quick peck on the cheek, but I pull her in for a kiss. I let my hand slowly move down her back and squeeze her ass, she jumps and brushes my hand away with a giggle. I watch as she walks out of the kitchen and into the front of the house towards our room. I could see the uncomfortable look on Nia's face as she watched me interact with Marissa, but I wasn't going to let it bother me she chose her position.

"It looks like the two of you are happy?" she says.

"We are," I reply, and she nods her head as she tries and musters up a fake smile.

"Look Brendan I didn't know that you were seeing someone. If I'd known I would've never just dropped by like this."

"What made you think that you could even if I wasn't seeing anyone."

She swallows hard and lowers her head. "I miss you, Brendan," she says and her voice cracking a little as she swallows back tears. "I made a mistake. I got impatient and you weren't giving me the time or the things that I needed."

"I gave you everything, what else did you want from me, Nia?" I say in a hard tone and she looks up at me tears filling her eyes.

"Kids, I wanted kids Brendan. But you were so focused on your practice and your patients that you were neglecting me and my needs." She said wiping the tears from her face. "You were so busy with your career that you couldn't even tell that I was no longer happy. Never once did you notice the change in my behavior, months had gone by and we hadn't even touched each other, and you hadn't noticed."

I was stunned because she was right. Now that I think back to those months before she's walked out we weren't having sex I mean we were barely speaking to each other. I just figured it was because I was always away from home and working late hours at the hospital. But she could've said something to me then, why wait until now? Fuck, why did she have to show up and dump all of this on me at this moment? I feel like a dick now that I've taken the time to listen to her reasoning because before I was so angry and hurt by the fact that she walked out on me that I was bitter, and I didn't want to hear anything that she had to say.

"I'm sorry, Nia," I said moving closer and placing my hand over hers. "I wish you would've talked to me before all of this. I never wanted to hurt you and never meant to neglect you the way that I did, I was so caught up in my own dreams and goals that I wasn't thinking of anyone or anything else. I should have noticed, and I should've taken the time to appreciate you and I didn't and I hope that you can forgive?"

"I have," She says in a low voice, "I love you Brendan and I'll always cherish what we had, and we did have a lot of great times together."

187

"Yeah, we did, didn't we?" I say offering her a smile and she does so in return.

"I'm happy that you found someone, and I can see that you two are in love with one another." She chuckles, "I don't think I've ever seen you look at anyone the way you look at her, not even me.

"She is an amazing woman,"

"Well I'm going to get out of your way, it's clear that you all were about to have dinner," She said getting up from her seat.

"I'll walk you out."

I walk her to her car and give her a quick embrace before opening her door for her. She climbs into the car and settles in her seat and I close the door waving to her one last time before heading back up the stairs towards the door. I rush inside and straight up to the master bedroom, Marissa was stretch out on the bed with the remote in her hand flipping through the channels.

"Hey baby, is everything ok?"

"Yeah, it is now," I say laying on the bed beside her pulling her in close. "I want you to promise me something."

"Ok, she said rolling over onto her side and gazing into my eyes. "what is it?" she asks stroking my hair with the tip of her fingers.

"Promise me that no matter what we go through or how hard things may get you'll always come to me so that we can talk about it."

Her eyes soften, and her lips turn up into a smile, "I promise."

I move closer so that I could kiss her, and she places her hand on my lips stopping me. "Uh-uh, if I plan on getting any food into this belly we're going to have to skip that and head back down to the kitchen." She says so I grab her hand and pull her over my shoulder as she let out a loud squeal.

Chapter Twenty

Marissa

Today is the grand reopening of the restaurant and I'm totally freaking out. We've been closed for nearly a month and a half and I'm praying that we didn't lose all of our customers to the new bar and grill that opened a block away. Brendan has really been a big help in keeping me sane during this whole process, and I really wish that he was here with me right now. But I understood that he needed to tend to his patients first. I walk through the kitchen one last time doubling checking with the chef and the kitchen staff making sure that everything was good to go before heading out to have a chat with my front of the house team.

Doors open in an hour and I would love for everything to go off without a hitch. The décor looked great and all of the colors in the dining area meshed well together. Making the space feel fun and family friendly. I finish making my rounds and head back to my office to take one last breather and get my head together before the crowd comes rushing in. I take out my phone and call my mother to check on the kids and then I try calling Brendan but no answer. I'm sure he's still pretty busy, it is nearing the end of the business day for him.

"Ms. Hopkins," a staff member says peeping in my office door.

"Yes?"

"There is a gentleman asking for you up front. Should I let him back?"

"Did he give a name?"

"No ma'am but I can go back and for it."

"No, no, it's fine. I'll be out in a second."

"Yes, ma'am," she says with a smile and walks out of the office.

I take one huge breath and exhale really slow before getting up from my seat. I straighten my skirt and fix my top before heading to the front of the house to see who this mystery man is that's asking for me. I reach the hall at the front entrance and see the tall, brown skinned, older man with salt and pepper colored hair standing by the door with his hands in his pocket.

"Dad?" I say as I approach him.

"Hello sweetheart," He says turning to face me.

"What are you doing here?"

"Oh, I just thought I'd stop by and see if you needed a hand?"

"Aw, dad you didn't have to do that." I say walking over and pulling him into a loving embrace.

"I know sweetie. I figured you and your staff might need some extra hands, so I brought mine." He said holding his hands up in front of him and wiggling his fingers.

I laugh and shake my head at him, "Come on old man I'm sure I can find something to do," I say tugging at his arm and he laughs.

"Hey, I'll have you know that I've got a lot of miles still left in this body young lady."

"Yeah, yeah I'm sure you do dad."

I have my dad help out with the front of the house staff while I take care of everything else. The hour flew by and before I knew it was time to open up and invite everyone in. The crowd outside of the restaurant was way more people than I'd imagined was going to show up for the re-opening. I stood at the door and greeted each and every one of the guest until the last one entered the restaurant. Everyone was so excited and shared how happy they were that we were back and how they'd missed the food. I was surprised to see all of Brendan's staff come walking through the door with him.

I greeted each of them and gave them a warm embrace before taking Brendan's hand and leading him back to my office. I shut the door and push back against it and press my lips and falling into a deep passionate kiss. He rips open my blouse and lifts me off the ground, walking over to my desk and placing me on top of it. I fumbled with his belt to get it loose then pull down his zipper and freeing his semi-erection.

"Wait, baby, I don't think we should do this now," he says into my mouth.

"Yes…now! I need you RIGHT NOW!"

I've wanted him since we woke up this morning and we haven't had sex in two days. I stroke his dick while he takes his time teasing my nipples with his tongue, grazing my erect nipples with his teeth sending me into a frenzy. Once he was hard and ready for me I lay back on the desk and spread my legs wide inviting him in. He steps forward and takes his dick into his hand, slowly rubbing the tip over my slit, parting my lips, and easing inside of me. I let out a low groan and tilt my hips forward lifting my ass off the desk allowing him to go

192

deeper. He grips my waist and plunges into me hard getting faster with each thrust.

"Omgosh...I'm coming baby,"

He lets out a low growl and pushing harder, deeper, and faster until we both completely lose it as my pussy squeezes his manhood tight. I crumble all around him as I feel him spasm and jerk inside of me releasing himself deep inside of me sending a wave of orgasms all through me. He falls forward placing his hand on each side of me on the desk. We stare at each other breathless with a huge smile on our faces.

"Have I told you how much I love you," He says leaning in and kissing me.

"Mm...I think you just did," I reply with a wink.

"Let's get cleaned up. You have a grand opening going on out there and I'm sure my friends are looking for me." He said helping me up from my desk.

We gather ourselves before leaving my office. I head over to check on how things are going with the staff, and he heads off to join his friends. The kitchen is running smoothly, and I've gotten nothing but positive feedback from each table that I've surveyed throughout the night. By closing we'd served over 300 people, my entire staff was exhausted by the end of the night but I'm proud of the work they'd done. They never slacked and were at the top of their game until the very end.

"Can you believe the crowd for tonight's opening," Karen asks looking up from her notepad.

"I know it was amazing," I reply taking a seat at my desk. "I honestly was not expecting everyone to show up."

"Great food and excellent service will always keep them coming back," she winks at me and continues writing on her notepad.

The staff swept through the store quickly cleaning and preparing for tomorrow night. Karen and I finished up the paperwork in my office then checked each station before everyone headed out. I sent a quick message to Brendan letting him know that I was on my way home and he sends back an eggplant emoji, drops of water, and a fist. My mouth drops and a smile spreads wide across my face I was happy to know that I wasn't the only one anticipating round two.

****

"Damn girl, you've been MIA for quite a while. I guess you've been enjoying Dr. Yummy on a more regular basis now." Belia laughs taking a sip of her wine. "I thought we'd lost you seeing as to how you completely abandoned your girls."

I laugh, "I'm sorry you guys. I've been busy and no not only with Brendan but the construction, the grand re-opening, and the kids. I've been exhausted."

"I'm proud of you," Trista said tipping her glass towards me. "Besides I hear Brendan has a brother, you may need to hook up your girl." She says winking at me.

"What…" Belia says. "Um, wait a minute what happen to your boo?" she asks as we both turn to look at Trista with a curious brow raised.

"Well…let's see I caught him making out with my neighbor's husband a few weeks ago during their football night." She replies.

"No way," I shout leaning forward in my chair because this was way too much tea.

"Shut up," Belia shouts. "Omgosh, I'm sorry you all but I knew he was gay. Everything about that man screamed put a dick in me." She says, and we burst out into a gut-busting laugh.

Even though we all knew that he was gay I kind of felt bad for Trista because she really liked him. I hate that she has such bad luck with men because she's such a sweet person. Hey, maybe I can talk to Brendan and set up a little get together and introduce the two of them. I mean hell why not his brother is a great catch and I wouldn't mind playing matchmaker for a day.

"So, did you kick him out?" I ask.

"Uh-hell yeah! Right on his ass, I told him to go shack up with his new boy toy." She replies.

"Well good for you doll," Belia says raising her glass and we both join in clinking our glasses together.

We continue our lunch and talk more about life and how things are going with each of us. I really wish that Nat had shown up but when I ask her to join us she waited an hour to respond then only sent back a simple "no thanks". I tried calling her a few times after the day she stopped by the house, but she hasn't answered any of my calls. I think I'll do a random drop by at her place so that I can talk to her and see what's going on with her. I mean we've had plenty of disagreements but never has she stopped talking to me. We finish up and say our goodbyes before heading our own separate ways.

195

I check on my staff and say a few words to Karen before leaving out for the day and head over to Natalie's. I pull into the driveway of her two-story townhouse and put the car in park before climbing out. I walk up to the door and ring the doorbell waiting patiently for her to open it. After a couple of seconds, the door swings open and Randy is standing in the doorway full nude.

"Oh gosh," I say raising my hands and covering my eyes. "Hi, Randy. Where's Natalie?"

"She's upstairs. Come in and I'll go get her for you," he says stepping to the side making room for me to pass.

"Thanks," I say stepping inside. "Do you always answer the door in the nude?" I ask with a hint of sarcasm in my tone.

"Uh yeah. I'm not really a shy person I've always been comfortable with nudity even as a kid." He chuckles.

I shake my head and give him an uneasy smile, I mean I really didn't know how to respond to that. "Well do you think that just for now you could go and put some pants on. I'm a little uncomfortable seeing my sister's boyfriend walking around with his junk hanging around."

"Ah, yeah sure. I'm sorry and I'll tell Natalie that you're here." He says turning on his heels to head up the stairs.

I take a seat on the sofa and wait for Natalie to come down from her room. The thought of his naked behind sitting on this very sofa made me cringe a little so I stood back up. From the look of things, it didn't seem like anything was unusual and he sure seemed to be settling into her life nicely. So, what is going on with her? After what seemed like

196

forever she finally came walking down the steps and into the living room.

"What do we not call before stopping by now?" She asks a hint of anger in her tone.

"Well, I would if a certain someone was answering my calls," I reply.

"Maybe the reason I'm not answering is because I don't want to talk." She rolls her eyes and takes a seat on the sofa.

I look at her for a minute studying her expression, trying to find a clue as to what is wrong with her. What I said that day wasn't really that bad, not bad enough for her to be mad or hate me for it. I mean it as our usual back forth so why was she being so distant and angry?

"Nat, what is going on with you," I begin taking the seat next t her, "If I said something that made you upset the last time we spoke I'm sorry."

"I'm pregnant," she blurts out and my breath catches in my throat.

"Um…Ok, well that's not what I was expecting." I say shocked. "But that's great Nat your going to be a mom—"

"But it's not Randy's," she says cutting me off and I look at her my face expressionless.

"What do you mean it's not Randy's? Does he know that?" I ask.

"No, he doesn't even know that I'm pregnant." She said pulling her knees to her chest and burying her face between them.

I sit back on the sofa puzzled trying to let my brain catch up and process everything that was being said. She'd come to tell me that she was pregnant that day she stopped by needing someone to listen and instead I was a complete jerk. No wonder she stormed out on me that day but wait a minute she'd cheated on Randy. But why? She's in love with him and everything was going so well with the two of them before Christmas.

"So, what are you going to do?" I ask

"I don't know, Marissa. I'm scared to tell him because I don't want to lose him." She sobs into her knees. "I made a mistake and now I'm probably going to lose the only man that's ever loved me since." She says then pauses and I knew exactly who she was referring to.

"It's going to be ok Nat," I say scooting closer and placing my arms around her shoulder. "Are you sure it's not his?"

"Yes," She says in between sobs. "I was sleeping with Kolby at the time of conception. Randy was out of town with his father when I got pregnant."

"Kolby," I say in a hard tone then realize that it's not the right time to criticize. "Have you been to the doctor?"

"Yes, they did an ultrasound and told me how far along I am. That's how I know that it's Kolby's and not Randy."

"Aw, Nat," I say hugging her tighter. "I'm so sorry sweetheart. You're going to have to tell him and you're going to need to call Kolby."

"I know," She replies.

198

"I'll be right there with you if you want me to. You don't have to do this alone, ok?" I say.

"Thanks, sis," she said offering me a weak smile, pulling me into an embrace.

I wait for her to gather herself and then have her call for Randy to come down so that she could break the news to him. After she explained to him about her ex from college coming into town and trying to rekindle an old flame he was upset. He never got angry or confrontational, but you could see that he was hurt by the things that she was saying. Once they were done talking he calmly packed his bags and kissed Natalie before leaving the house. I could only imagine the way that he was feeling, and I understand his reason for leaving but I also respect him for not flying off the handle. She called Koby and set up a lunch date for tomorrow so that she could tell him about the baby. I told her that I would go along with her, but she told me that she would be ok to do it alone. I didn't know much about the Kolby now, but the Kolby that I use to know was a great guy and if he's half the guy he was then he'll do the right thing and step up no matter what.

Chapter Twenty-One

Brendan

Today was my day to hang out with Jasmine and Josh. You know have some bonding time with just the three of us, so I decided to take them with me to shop for an engagement ring. That way I could ask them how they would feel about me asking their mom to marry me. I take them for ice cream first just so that we could sit down in a quiet space and talk before heading to the jewelry store.

"What flavor ice cream would you like Princess Jasmine?" I ask.

"I want strawberry and chocolate," She says twisting her foot at the heel with her arms behind her back.

"Alright, a scoop of each it is. What about you Josh, what flavor would you like?" I say turning to face him.

"I think I'll have…Chocolate," He said after giving it a little thought.

"OK," I say before turning to the guy behind the counter and placing our order.

We take our ice cream and go over to one of the small tables with three chairs that's off to itself and take our seats. Jasmine digs right in filling her mouth with a huge spoon full of ice cream after a couple of seconds her little face scrunches up and she squeezes her eye's shut wiggling her head. She'd gotten a brain freeze and Josh and I laughed at the expression on her face. I hand her my bottle of water and have her take a sip since it was room temper and placed her tongue at the roof of her mouth for a few seconds.

"So, I want to ask you guys a question, is that ok?" I asked, and they nodded their heads yes. "Ok, well I want to know how the two of you feel about me and your mom being together?"

"You mean as boyfriend and girlfriend?" Josh asks.

"Yes," I reply.

"I think it's cool. I like seeing my mom happy and I like having a guy around to talk to about you know guy stuff."

"And I like having you around Brendan because I love you," Jasmine chimes in.

"Aw, I love you too Princess Jasmine," I reply reaching over and pinching her cheek and she smiles big and wide.

I'd fallen in love with her kids in a very short time and I can't see myself living a day without them in my life already. I know that I can't take the place of their dad and I would never try to, but I do want to be the best man and father figure that I can be. I want to be there to watch them grow up and be there for all of their up's, downs, first dates, first kisses, proms, graduations, and everything else that comes along with it.

"Well you know I was sort of thinking that I would ask your mom to marry me." I begin and they both turn to look at me, the expression that came across both of their faces and the beaming smiles pretty much gave me my answer, but I still wanted to wait for their answer.

"Are you serious?" Josh asks.

"Of course, I love your mom very much and I would love to be in you all's life forever," I reply.

"Yay, mommy and Mr. Brendan are getting married," Jasmine shouts and everyone in the shop looks over at us.

"So is that ok with the two of you,"

"Yes!" They both shout in unison before leaping out of their seats and rushing me, wrapping their arms around me and squeezing me tight.

We finish our ice cream then head into town to one of my favorite Jewelry stores. I take the kids inside and greet my long-time friend Nicholas and owner of the store. He shows me his collection of engagement rings and I pick out a few that I feel best suit Marissa then I have the kids help me make my final decision. We finally decide on a princess cut diamond halo ring set, Nicholas nodded in agreement then headed off to ready the ring. He returned a couple of minutes with the ring placed in a red box and checked us out.

"Now you to have to keep quiet because it's a surprise, ok?"

"Yes sir," They both reply nodding their heads.

"No spilling the beans Jazzy," Josh said pointing his finger at his sister.

"Hey...I'm not. Leave me alone buttface." She says and sticks her tongue out at him.

"Alright you guys come on let's head home," I say taking Jasmine's hand as we exit the store and head to the car.

****

I get both of our parents together and tell them about my planned proposal, and let me tell you, I use to think that my mother was over the top. No, her mother is dramatic, in a good kind of way. But the both of them together is a bit overwhelming, I couldn't get my mother to stop crying and my soon to be mother-in-law was shouting for the rest of the night. My father was happy, and I felt it only right to ask her father if he was alright with it, and he pats me on the shoulder and said, "Oh, I believe you'll fit in around here just fine son". Our parents connected so well and the chemistry between the four was effortless that I knew things were going to be great. And my mother was happy that she was finally going to have some grandbabies running around the place.

I had Janice call and book a party at her restaurant for Saturday night so that we would have the place all to ourselves. I didn't want her to catch on to the surprise, so I didn't want to call myself and have someone recognize my voice. Everyone knew their part and what they were supposed to do leading up to the night. Now all I have to do is get through the rest of the week without having a panic attack and wimp out before then.

"Brendan, you got a second?"

"Hey Dawn, yeah come in," I say closing my laptop.

"Can you take a look at this CT and tell me what you see?" She asks still waiting by the door.

"Sure, let's go have a look," I say getting up from my seat and following her down the hall. "Is there something that you're not sure about on the images?"

"I think I'm fairly certain, but I just want to have another set of eyes take a look before I head over to the hospital." She replies as we turn the corner and enter the small room.

She walks over and puts up the images up and I step closer to examine them up close. She waits silently why I check each one carefully looking for anything unusual then I pause mid-step and turn to her.

"Has this person had any head trauma?" I ask, and she smiles.

"I knew it," she says stepping closer. "Take a look at this. The patient said she'd been pushed out of a moving car and suffered significant head trauma and she'd gone to the ER for treatment, but they sent her home and told her that she was fine." She says, and I nod my head for her to go on. "So, I sent over a request for the images from the ER and this is what they sent back." She moves to the other side and I follow along.

"That's not possible," I say looking at the images. "Dawn, I think you have a case of medical malpractice on your hands."

"I think so," She says pulling the images and turning off the screen. "Thanks, Brendan, I'm going to head over to the hospital so that I can talk to the director."

"Alright, keep me posted and let me know if you need me to make some calls," I say, and she nods to me before heading out of the room.

I don't know who that young lady is but she's going to be a very rich woman once this gets to the board. There is no way they are going to let this make it to the courts they'll try and pay her off in exchange for her silence. Hopefully, she's one of the strong ones and pushes to take them to court anyway. Because that hospital has screwed over its fair share of patients through the years and someone needs to stop them. I'm confident that Dawn will give her the best advice and have her contact a great lawyer.

I leave the office early and head home so that I could get ready for dinner tonight with Marissa, my brother, and her best friend Trista. She told me about her friend's situation with the last guy she was dating and how she wanted to help so I agreed. I mean they're both single so why not give it a try. Although I'm not sure if this little hook up is going to work because my brother is more of a blonde haired, big boobs kind of guy. And her friend Trista is petite, brown skinned, long sandy brown hair, and honey colored eyes. I've never seen him turn a woman down based on her looks so I'm sure he'll give her a fair chance, but what do I know maybe they'll connect mentally.

"Baby, is that you?" Marissa calls down from our room.

"Yes, sorry I'm late there was a lot of traffic," I say putting away my things.

"It's ok, I laid your clothes out on the bed for you like you asked and your brother said he's on his way there now."

I walk into the closet and find her searching through her dresses with nothing but a pair of red lace panties on. My dick twitches to attention and I stand watching her until she turns around and looks at me.

"What?" She asks with a wide smile.

"I'm just admiring the view. Please continue," I say with a wink.

205

She walks over to me and kisses me, "Later," she says then rubs her hand over the front of my pants caressing my manhood.

"Not if you keep that up," I say smacking her on the ass as she walks back over to the dresses.

I take a quick shower and get dressed and join her downstairs where she's waiting for me with her friend on the sofa. She must have arrived while I was in the shower because I didn't hear the buzzer for the front gate. Her friend looked stunning and I was rather surprised at how beautiful she looked, I don't think I would've recognized her if we were just in passing. She usually looks rather plain any other time that she's come around.

"Are you ladies ready to go?" I ask and they both turn to me beaming.

"Yes, we are," Marissa said getting up from the sofa and walking over taking my arm.

We head out to the SUV where Ahmad is waiting for us and I help each of the ladies inside before taking my seat next to Marissa. We wait patiently while Ahmad heads around to the driver's side and claims his seat then pulls away from the house. Kyle was already inside waiting for us at the table when we arrived. Once inside the hostess showed us to the table and Kyle stood to greet us as we approached the table. When he notices that the beautiful young woman walking beside us was actually his date I could see the nervous look in his eyes immediately turn to lust. He was attracted to her so that was a good sign. Now let's see if they show any signs of chemistry and connection on a deeper level.

"Kyle, it's nice to see you," Marissa says walking up and giving him a warm embrace.

"What's up bro," he says giving my quick fist bump.

"Kyle, I would like for you to meet my best friend Trista," Marissa says as they step over closer to a trembling Trista.

"It's nice to meet you, Trista," Kyle says leaning in and kissing her on the cheek.

"Pleasure," She begins, "Wow, you two are actually Identical like in every sense of the word."

"Yeah, well at sept for the fact that I'm older and a bit wiser," He says, and I chuckle.

"You may be two minutes older but I'm clearly the better looking and way smarter," I say and we all laugh then take our seats.

We kept the conversation light and free-flowing so that Trista could relax some. I could tell that she was nervous when we sat down, so I figured our crazy sense of humor would break the ice and it did. We joked around a little before changing the subject to something that would let them get to know more about each other. The waitress came over and took our order and returned with our drinks several minutes later. We continued our conversation until the food arrived.

"So, Kyle are you in the medical field as well?" Trista asks.

"No, I've never had the right kind of patience that it takes to become a doctor," he replies.

"Oh, so what do you have the patience for?" She says with a flirtatious smile and Kyle catches on to it quickly.

"I'm more of a brainy kind of guy," he laughs. "I own a tech company that I'm sure you've probably heard of seeing as to how you have one of our phones."

She looks down at the table then back up at him, "Are you serious, you created this?"

"Well me and a team of other people," Kyle replies.

"Omgosh…that's amazing! I work in the tech industry as well."

"Do you now," Kylie asks his interest now peeked.

"Yes, I'm the VP of marketing and advertising for a tech company."

"Amazing," Kyle smiles, "You are absolutely amazing." He says staring at her with that same look that I have when I look at Marissa.

And just like that, we knew that the two of them had connected. Marissa looks over at me and winks then rubs her hand over my thigh smiling at me and I lean in and put my arm around her so that I could whisper in her ear.

"You're being a very naughty girl. Maybe I should take you to the restroom and give you a good spanking," I say in a hard-sexy tone and she giggles.

"Ready when you are," she whispers into my ear letting her tongue brush across neck before kissing it.

Our playful banter gets the other twos attention and Kyle clears his throat drawing our focus back to them. He looks at me with a raised brow and Trista giggles into her hand as she watches the two of us.

208

"You two are like two lovesick teens, it's disgusting," Kyle says with a grunt and I flip him my middle finger.

"So, on that note, I think we're going to call it an evening," Trista says winking at Marissa.

"I agree," Marissa says looking over at me biting her bottom lip.

When the waiter arrives with the bill Kyle insists on paying the check and eventually I give in and let him have his way. The three of us head outside while he takes care of the check and wait for him to join us. We give each other one last hug and say our goodbyes before heading off to the SUV. Kyle turns back and calls out to us just as we begin to walk away.

"Trista, do you mind if I give you a ride home?" Kyle asks and her face lights up.

"Uh—no, of course. If it's not too much trouble," She replies.

"It's not," He grins, "Besides it'll give the two of them some privacy and a little more time for the two of us to talk."

"Great," She says then turns around and hugs Marissa then me and says a final goodnight before heading off with my brother.

Marissa and I walk over to where Ahmad is parked and climb into the SUV and take our seats cuddling close. I'm happy with how everything turned out and it was nice to see my brother looking so hopeful. He's a really good guy but he's had some really shitty experiences in the relationship department. But I think things will turn out great for the two of them.

"I think that went, well don't you?" she asks.

"Yeah, they really hit off," I reply.

"You did good cupid," I say, and she laughs then leans in to kiss me.

As soon as we walked in the door we were ripping each other's close off and leaving them wherever they landed. I pick her up into my arms and carry her up the steps to our bedroom and that's where we remained for the rest of the night making love.

Chapter Twenty-Two

Marissa

I've spent the entire morning hurled over the toilet puking my brains out. I rarely ever get sick and this week is the worst possible time. We have a huge party booked at the restaurant this week and the couple is requesting my presence on that night. I really don't know how I'm going to make it through the longest I can go is maybe twenty minutes before I'm hurling all over again. Brendan called to see if I wanted to grab lunch and that when I told him I've been sick the majority of the day. He tells me to come into the office so that he can have a look but I'm not sure if I want to try and drive, so I call up Belia to drive me.

"Hey girl," Belia says after the second ring.

"Hey," I say back but my voice barely goes above a whisper because I'm so weak.

"What's wrong love?" She asked.

"I'm not feeling so well can you give me a ride to the doctor's office."

"Sure, I'll be over in a jiffy," she says and quickly hangs up.

I slowly pull on a pair of sweatpants and a loose shirt before struggling to get my sneakers on. My head starts to swim so I sit back on to the bed for a second before trying to get up again. As I reach the bottom step Belia rings the door boor and I pull on my coat and grab my purse before opening the door.

"Oh, babe, you look like hell,"

"Gee thanks are you just a breath of fresh air," I say in a sarcastic tone.

"I'm sorry. Here let me help you."

She takes my arm into hers and helps me down the stairs and over to the car opening the door for me and I get inside. I wasn't really in the mood for conversation and she could tell so we road quietly until we reached Brendan's clinic. I tried my best to focus on something other than the motion of the car because every bump and turn is torture. She pulls up to the door and gets out to help me inside and after I get in she helps me to my seat then goes back out to park the car.

The nurse calls my name just a couple of seconds later and I slowly make my way to the back. Once we get into the room she closes the door behind us and goes straight over to the computer. After a series of questions, she takes my vitals and sends me to collect a urine sample. I hadn't really thought much about my period until she'd asked me the date of my last cycle and that's when I realized that I'm late. "Oh fuck, I'm late," I say to myself as I look into the mirror holding onto the sink to keep myself balanced. I begin to feel dizzy again, so I turn on the cold water and splashed my face a couple of times. Could I be pregnant? No, there's no way my periods only a couple of days late and I've been really stressed lately so that probably why.

I place the cup inside the little window and go back to the room and climb onto the table and lay back closing my eyes.

There's a knock at the door after a while and in walks the lady doctor with my file in her hand.

"Good Afternoon, Ms. Wilmore," She says in welcoming tone.

"Hello," I reply.

"My name is Dawn and I'll be the physician caring for you today. So, I hear you've had a bit of nausea and vomiting, how long has that been going on?"

"Yesterday I was feeling a little tired and sluggish then today I just couldn't keep anything down."

"And your periods have they been pretty regular?" She questions.

"Uh…yeah," I begin, "Well kind of it's actually a couple of days late." I sigh.

"I see," She said. "So, let's see what the results of your pregnancy test are and then we will go from there." She smiles and gets up from her seat.

She walks out the door and I fall back onto the table placing my hands on my stomach. Could there be a little mini Brendan growing inside me? My lips pull up into a smile at the thought of a baby boy that has all of Brendan's features running around. But what will happen if I am I mean we haven't really discussed kids, so I don't know if its something that he wants. I mean he's great with Jasmine and Josh. He adores them, and he's accepted them as if they were his very own but what if he's not ready to add another kid. Just as the panic sets in the door opens to my room and Brendan walks in and closes the door. He's holding a folder

213

in his hand and the look on his face made my stomach begin to turn flips.

He clears his throat and places the folder on the table then scoots over to the exam table taking my hands into his.

"You are freaking me out, Brendan. Is there something wrong?" I ask my voice panicked and shaky.

"Marissa, you're pregnant," He says and suddenly the room closes in on me and the air gets thick as my eyes filled with tears. "Breath baby," he said standing up and pulling me into his arms.

I close my eyes and take in slow steady breaths as he strokes my back with one hand. Once I regained control I opened my eyes and looked up at him and he was staring back at me with a smile on his face that touched his eyes.

"You're not mad," I ask.

He chuckles, "Mad? Marissa, why would I be mad at you?"

"I—I don't know," I say stumbling over my words. "I mean we've never talked about kids, were not married, and I don't even know if we're ready for another kid. Are you ready for another kid?" I question.

"Marissa, baby, calm down," he says taking his seat again. "I told you I want to spend the rest of my life with you, with a house full of babies,"

"Whoa—I think one more will be enough,"

"Mm…two," he says quickly.

"Ok, but only two," I say, and he smiles up at me then stands and lifts me off the table and into his arms and starts to kiss me, but I raise my hand and put it over my mouth.

"Oh, no, babe. That's probably not a good idea I haven't brushed my teeth" I say, and he laughs then kisses the top of my head.

"I love you, Marissa,"

"I love you more,"

I wait for the nurse to come back and bring me the information that Brendan had her print up. She hands me the papers with the information to an OBGYN, that just so happens to be a good friend of Brendan's then I head to the checkout desk. I step into the waiting room and walk over to Belia who was seated in the corner flipping through a magazine.

"Hey chic, I'm all done."

"Great, so what did they say? Is it flu?" She asks curiously.

"Not quite," I say scrunching my face up and placing my hand on my belly.

"Shut the front door," she said catching herself as she looked around the waiting room. "Are you serious?" She whispers, and I nod my head at her and she does a little dance in place.

"Shh..." I say pulling her towards the exit. "Come on I'll talk to you about it in the car."

As we ride back to my house I think of all the ways that I can share the news about the baby with the kids. I'm sure my parents will be happy and his mother, oh gosh, his mother is going to be ecstatic to hear the news. I'm going to have to think of an extra special way to surprise his parents since this is a really big moment being that it's their first grandbaby.

Belia drops me back off at home and I head inside to take a hot bath before I lie down to take a nap, so I'll be rested once Brendan and the kids get home.

****

Brendan asks me and the kids to move in with him since we're basically living with him anyway. We barely stay in our house anymore and the drive to the restaurant is a lot shorter from here. And still, I had to really think about whether or not I wanted to give up the house that held so many memories for me and the kids. Chandler and I bought that house right after we were married, and my children have grown up in that house. But after much thought and a very long talk with Brendan, we both concluded that both homes were always going to hold memories of our past lives, and the loves that we lost while in them. So, we agreed to purchase a new home together and have our own little beginning. A place where we'll start our family and create new memories with one another.

It didn't take long for us to find a home that we both thought to be perfect for our growing family. Even though we both agreed that it needs a bit of a touch up to make it more suitable for us, so we hired a contractor for a quick upgrade. And hopefully, in a couple of months we'll be able to settle into our new home but for now, we'll settle for his place.

The babysitter arrives, and I gather my things, hug the kid's goodbye, then head off to the restaurant. We have an extremely big party tonight, and the guy bought out the entire restaurant as a surprise for his fiancée. I rush inside and find everyone is already hard at work. The tables and chairs have been moved and the place was overflowing with flowers, candles, and beautiful decor. It was amazing, whoever this gentlemen's fiancé is, she's a very lucky woman.

Everything was set, and the food was done and in place. I could hear the people as they arrived, and the soft music begins to play. I did one last walk through to make sure that everything was up to par, I wanted everything to be perfect for our special guest.

I head to my office area in the back of the restaurant and change into the dress that my children suggested I wear tonight for my big event. Now that I think about it they seemed a little too excited about it all. I check my hair again in the small mirror hanging in the corner of my office and quickly touch up my make-up. I hear a knock at the door, I open it and find my mom standing there with this ridiculously cheesy smile.

"Mom!" I shout.

"Hello, darling." She says pulling me into a full embrace.

"What are you doing here? Is everything ok?"

"Of course, sweetheart. Your dad and I just came for dinner."

"Aw, mom. I'm sorry, but the restaurant is closed for a private party tonight."

"I know, we were invited." She says smiling at me with a very weird expression on her face. "Come with me sweetheart I have someone I'd like you to meet."

She takes my arm and leads me through the kitchen. We reach the double doors and she stops, steps in front of me, and looks me in the eyes. "I just want to say that I'm so proud of you and I love you so very much." She mumbles tearing up a little and I couldn't help but be confused by this moment that we were having right now.

"Thanks, mom. And I love you too."

We walk out into the room and I see all of my family, friends, and employees, both the ones working and the ones that were not.

"What's going on?" I ask looking over at my mother who had tears streaming down her face. I turn my focus back to the smiling crowd and finally notice Brendan, standing in the middle of the crowd with a bouncing Jasmine and Josh grinning from ear to ear. My mom releases me, and I walk over to them.

"What's going on you guys?" I ask.

"Mom, it's your party. Surprise!" Jasmine yells out, jumping up and down in place smiling.

"Party?" I say looking from my son to Brendan, with a raised eyebrow.

He smiles back at me, releasing my daughter's hand and slowly moves closer to me and takes a knee. At that moment I realized exactly what was going on, and a flood of emotions washed over me, I lift my hands to my face as tears cloud my eyes. He reaches out to take my hand and I reach out and place it into his.

"Marissa Wilmore, you are such an amazing woman and I can't see myself going another day without making you, my wife. I want to spend each and every day waking up with you and falling asleep with you next me wrapped in my arms every night. I want to raise our kids together, grow old, and take every step leading into my future with you right by my side. So, I ask, Marissa, will you do me the honor of becoming Mrs. Hopkins?"

I fall to my knees in front of him and wrap my arms around him, hugging him tightly, crying into his shoulder. "Yes, Yes, I'll marry you," I say kissing him as we both get back up on to our feet. He slides the Princes cut Halo Diamond engagement ring on my finger, as everyone cheers, and my kids run over and hug me tight. They'd known all along, that was why they were so excited about the party happening tonight.

Chapter Twenty-Three

Brendan

She said YES!

The night has been great, and the proposal was a success, we'd pulled it off and she had absolutely no clue. I have to admit though I was afraid that Jasmine was going to let it slip a few times, but she kept her promise and didn't spill the beans as Josh would say. On top of that finding out that she's pregnant with my child makes this moment that more special. When the results of her test came back I was shocked. Although there were a few times in the heat of the moment that we didn't use protection and asking if she was on birth control hadn't really crossed my mind. Nonetheless I'm happy to have Marissa be the mother of my child, she's an amazing woman and she's proven that she's a great mom.

We still have not broken the news to the kids yet but I'm sure they'll be excited to have another brother or sister. As for my parents, I have a fairly good idea of how that conversation is going to go, a lot of tears and high pitch screams from my mother. She's going to be plotting ways to spoil this kid rotten before it even exits the womb. We'd decided to tell everyone at the same time and I suggested this weekend since my parents were already in town. We're going to play it off like it's a simple gathering you know a family night before my parent's head back home. Her best friend Belia already knew so we had her help us out with all the planning and she'll help with the reveal.

Marissa bought a few baby things that she's going to wrap as gifts and give to my parents, her parents, and the kids. We're going to record the surprise so that she can add it to the baby's box of memories. I can't believe that I'm going to be a father there was once a time when kids scared the hell out of me. Kids were never a part of my future plans, but I believe now that is because I hadn't found the right woman.

My father and I spend some time at the gun range with Marissa's father Chance. He likes to go and shoot whenever he wants to relax, strange to me how shooting a gun is relaxing, but I was all for it. I'd never held a gun or shot one before, so I was intrigued and eager to have a go at it. Everyone greeted Chance by name as we entered the Range so I'm guessing he comes to let off steam a lot.

"So, Carl, what's it going to be?" Mr. Wilmore asked standing in front of the case that displayed an array of handguns.

"I think I'll take the Glock," my father says, and I look at him with a raised brow.

"Nice choice my man," he replies then looks over at me.

"I'll take the Smith & Wesson," I say pointing the chrome 9mm.

After we make our selection we follow Carl to the back and he shows us to the room where we'll be shooting. He hands us a pair of soundproof headphones to put on before we walk into the room. After we get situated and, in our spot, Carl steps up and places his gun on a small table in front of him. He stretches his hands and his arms a few times before picking it back up. He presses the button on his right sending his target back into position then aims and begins to fire.

221

His aim was on point and every round either hit the middle of the page or went straight through the head. Let's just say that I will have to watch my back if things ever go sour between Marissa and me.

My father steps up next and Carl sends down a fresh target for my father as he picks up his gun. Once Carl stepped back my father aimed his gun and begin to let off a few rounds. When the sheet moved closer I could see my father had made every shot to the middle of the target and one to the head.

"Uh…dad, I think you and I need to have a conversation so that you can tell me when and how you learned to shoot like that." I say, and my father lets out a chesty laugh.

"I learned a lot of things back in my younger days son," He replies stepping out of the box and patting me on the shoulder.

I step up next and ready myself before he presses the button sending my target down the line then move back next to my father. I take a deep breath and relax my shoulders before letting it rip and the rush that I got from pumping out each and every round was exhilarating. The adrenaline rush was kind of a turn on and at that moment I couldn't wait to get home and tell Marissa all about it. We upgraded after a while and even got a little bet going once everyone got comfortable and loose. Once we left the Range we were all amped up and on a high that felt great. My father chooses his favorite restaurant that he loves to visit when he's here in town, and lunch was on Mr. Wilmore since my father won their little bet. Kyle met up with us at the restaurant for lunch since he missed out on going to the Range. He'd gotten a call from his office and had to rush off to handle his business before meeting back up with us.

"How are things going with Trista?" I ask Kyle while gaining a side glance from Mr. Wilmore.

"It's going great," Kyle says shooting me a death stare and I chuckle as Carl chimes in.

"You been seeing Marissa's best friend son?" Carl asks.

"Yes sir," Kyle replies.

"She's a really sweet girl and very special to me. You better treat her good son." Carl says in a hard tone.

"Oh, I plan to sir," Kyle replies before nudging me in the arm.

We order our food and talk more while we wait for the waitress to return with our drink orders. The conversation was flowing smoother than a glass of whiskey, and Carl had us all laughing so hard that my abs here on fire by the time we finished up our meal. We drove back to the house still laughing and joking the same as we were at the restaurant. As we entered the house the ladies were seated in the living room indulging in their own conversation laugh and having a good time with one another.

My father goes over and kisses my mother as Carl and I follow suit going over and kissing our women. Our kiss lasted a bit longer than everyone else's quick peck on the lips that is until we noticed all the little giggles.

"Alright son, the two of you can come up for air now," My father says and everyone in the room burst into laughter.

I pull Marissa up from the chair that she was seated in then pulled her down into my lap. She gets comfortable and puts her arms loosely around my neck then joining back in on the conversation.

****

Being stuck in meetings all morning and with a migraine is a pain in the ass. I pour myself a cup of water and grab the bottle of painkillers from my bag and pop two into my mouth. I need relief and fast or I'm going to have to excuse myself from the rest of my meetings that I have this evening. I go back into the room and take my seat listening to the Senior VP of the hospital finishing speaking. As he comes to an end he introduces me, and I nod to the others at the table before making my way to the front of the room. After I go over my plans and give my full proposal to the board, I take questions and we get down to business.

Walking out at the end of the day I felt great. Partnering up with this hospital has been something that I've been working towards for a long time. I can't wait to see what the future holds for us all and for my staff and colleges as well. I had the rest of the day off, so I head over to the restaurant to meet up with Marissa, so we could finish going over plans for tonight's baby announcement to our families. Natalie revealed her pregnancy just a week ago to her parents and tonight it's our turn. Two baby announcements in less then a week I'm pretty sure her parent's heads are going to spinning.

"Hey baby you're home early," Marissa says walking over and giving me a quick kiss on lips.

"Yep. Everything ran smoothly this morning and by the end, they were begging to sign my proposal."

"That's great baby," She says hugging once more.

"So, what is it that you need for your loving fiancé to do to help you?" I ask smacking her on her ass.

"Brendan," she squeaks.

"What? It's mine," I chuckle.

"Not in front of my staff baby," she says in a low voice and I grab it again. She jumps and turns smacking my hand away. "Behave," she says trying to keep a straight face.

Once she's finished taking care of her business we head out to get the shopping done before picking up the kids and heading home.

Chapter Twenty-Four

Marissa

I'm so excited to tell my family about our new bundle of joy but I'm also a bit nervous to see the kids reaction. Even though they've never asked for another sibling I'm about ninety-five percent sure they're going to be just as excited as we are. We'd spent most of yesterday shopping and preparing for tonight's dinner with our family and I'm really amazed by how attentive Brendan is being. I wasn't expecting him to be so excited but he's over the moon about the baby.

"Let me do that for you baby," He says coming over and pulling the roast out of the oven.

"Thanks, babe," I reply going over and taking a seat on the stool in front of the breakfast nook.

"Are you feeling ok? You look kind of pale."

"I'm just tired," I say giving him a weak smile.

"Maybe you should take a nap before everyone arrives," He says coming over and sitting next to massage my shoulders.

"No, babe, I don't want to put all of this on you,"

"You're not Belia will be here soon. She'll help me finish up, go on get some rest." he kisses me on the forehead and I slide out of my seat and head up to our room.

This is all new to me I didn't have morning sickness or anything with Jasmine or Josh so I'm hoping that this is only an in the beginning thing. I can't imagine trying to run a restaurant or any kind of business if I'm hurling each and every moment of the day. I climb into the bed and adjust my pillow to get comfortable then lay my head on the pillow and close my eyes.

I'm not sure how long I was out but when I woke it felt like hours. I felt better the Nausea was gone and no more dizziness. I sat up and stretched my arms high in the air and yawned deeply before getting out of bed and going to the restroom. I hadn't noticed any wetness or moister when I got out of the bed but when I looked down there was blood in the lining of my panties. My heart dropped from my chest and it felt like someone had sucked the air out of my lungs.

"Omgosh.... what is happening?" I say to myself slowly standing up and cleaning myself off.

A sob escapes me, and I fall to the floor, I needed Brendan, and I tried to call out to him, but I couldn't get my voice to go any louder from the sobbing. I think I sat on the floor for at least five minutes before I gained enough strength to call out for someone. I hear footsteps and then a knock on the door, it's Brendan.

"Marissa, are you ok baby?" He asks.

"No," I sob. "Brendan, help me, please help me."

He opens the door and rushes over to me kneeling down beside me. "What's wrong?" he asks examining me and finally noticing the blood on my shorts. "Oh shit, baby I need you to stand up for me. Are you having any pain?" He asks trying to help me off the floor, but I couldn't stand so he scoops me into his arms.

He carries me out of the room and rushes down the stairs calling out to Belia for her to grab my purse and the cars and meet us at the car.

"What's wrong? Brendan, what happened?" She shouts.

"It's the baby. I'll call you from the hospital," he says.

"What do you want me to tell everyone?"

"Nothing. Just tell them something important came up and we'll be back soon." He yells from the car as he helps me inside then rushes to the other side and gets into the car.

He speeds out of the drive and down the street heading to the hospital. He calls up his friend, and my OB, to have him meet us at the ER. I sat holding my belly and saying a silent pray until he pulled up to the curb at the ER. He rushed inside and comes back with two nurses and a wheelchair. The nurse quickly swung open the car door and Brendan lifted me out of the seat and into the wheelchair. Once we were in the room he helps me out of my clothes and into a gown while the nurse takes my information. After they take my vitals and get my IV started they leave us alone to wait for the doctor.

"Brendan, I'm so scared," I say in a low voice.

"I know baby, but it's going to be ok don't worry."

"What if we lose the baby?"

"Let's not think like that," He replies scooting his chair closer to me and taking my hand kissing the back of it.

"Ms. Wilmore," Dr. Rowan says stepping into the room and shaking hands with Brendan. "So, I hear you're having some bleeding and discomfort. Is that right?"

"Yes," I say my voice barely a whisper.

"And when did you notice the bleeding?" He asks.

"Just a while ago when I woke up from a nap," I reply.

"I see," he says walking over to me and lifting my gown so that he could examine my abdomen. "is there any pain or pressure when I touch here?"

"No," I reply.

"And what about here?" He says.

"No, just light cramping," I respond.

"Alright, I'm going to order an ultrasound so that we can take a look and figure out what's going on." He says as he pats me on the leg. "Don't worry we're going to take good care of you."

"Thanks, Dominic," Brendan says, and he smiles and gives a slight nod before leaving out the room.

About twenty minutes later they take me to another room where I wait to have my ultrasound. Dr. Rowan walks in with a nurse trailing behind him and she closes the door behind them. "So, let's take a look and see what's going on inside there," he says prepping the ultrasound tool so that he could perform it vaginally. My body tenses a little as he slowly pushes it inside of me.

"Try and relax for me, Marissa," He says in a calm and relaxing tone and I shake my head.

229

Brendan takes my hand in his and holds it tight and the touch of his hand helps me relax almost immediately. I look up at him and he smiles down at me, he was being so strong for me, but I could see in his eyes that he was nervous as well. The doctor moved the wand around for what seemed like forever and I could feel the panic growing in me more and more with each passing second. And the agonizing silence in the room was only making it worse, then finally he says something.

"Ah there we go," he says reaching for the button and turning up the sound. "Your babies heartbeats," he says smiling over at the two of us.

Tears sting my eyes and I turn to Brendan and squeeze his hand, I was so relieved to hear that tiny thump and the little jelly bean image on the screen. Then suddenly the expression on Brendan's face changes and I turn to look at the screen.

"Uh…Dominic what's that?" he asks swallowing hard. "Is that—"

"Well I'll be, look at that. Congratulations, looks like the two of you are going to have twins," He says clicking the keyboard to take a few images.

A nervous laugh escapes me, "Twins?" I ask focusing harder on the screen and finally, I see the second little jelly bean image appear. "Oh my gosh. Brendan, we're having twins," I say my voice still shaky and he leans in and kisses me, excitement filling his eyes.

He removes the wand and steps out of the room so that I could clean myself off then he comes back into the room. He hands me the images of the babies and then takes a seat at the computer.

"So, everything is fine with the babies. Their hearts are beating strong and everything on the ultrasound looked great." He says and then his face takes a more serious expression as he leans against the counter. "Now bleeding can accrue when one is carrying twins and when that happens that only means that we need to take caution. So, I'll see you every two weeks over the next couple of months for an ultrasound. I've also noticed that your stress levels seem to be a bit high, so I'm going to need you to take it easy for a while until we get you through the second trimester." He says with a nod.

"So, no work?" I ask.

"No work," He smiles.

"Ok," I reply and return the smile.

I wasn't thrilled to hear that but whatever I have to do to keep my babies safe I'm going to do it. Brendan helps me get dressed in a pair of scrub bottoms that the nurse brought me since my shorts were bloodstained. Then once the discharge papers were ready he wheeled to the front of the hospital and we waited as the valet brought the car around.

We pull into the garage, and he helps me out of the car. We go in the side door so that we wouldn't run into anyone as we entered the house. He's called Belia once we left the hospital to let her know that we were on our way back. She made sure that everyone was in the living room once we arrived so that we would have a clear shot through the kitchen and up to our room. I change into a fresh pair of clothes and then we head downstairs to join the rest of our family.

"There the two of you are," Natalie says walking over to me and pulling me into a hug. "You know that two of you work

absolutely way too much, you need to learn to call in sick."
She winks and kisses me on the check.

"Is everything ok?" My mother asks looking at me with a
curious look in her eye.

"Yes, everything is fine," Brendan speaks up, moving closer,
and placing one arm around my waist.

"Well come on over and have a seat," His mother says
motioning us over.

We walk over and sit next to each other on the couch and
Belia brings over three gifts and handed them to me.
Everyone was watching us with a confused look on their face
and Brendan and I look at each other and smile. I hand him
the gifts then nod to him, he gets up from his seat and hands
one to the kids, another to my parents, and one to his parents.
They take the boxes into their hands and fumbles them
around.

"What's this mom?" Josh asks.

"We have something that we'd like to share with you all
before we have dinner," Brendan says as he walks back over
and takes his seat beside me.

"Open them," I say, and they rip into the paper.

My mother gets hers open first and she looks up from the box
at the two of us then back down again. She covers her mouth
with her hand and her eyes well up with tears. My father
reaches over and pulls the baby bottle and rattle out of the
box and looks over at us smiling. His parents get theirs open
next and his mother lets out a loud squeal and pops up and
down in her seat reaching over and hugging Mr. Hopkins.

"Omgosh, Marissa," Natalie shouts.

"No way, bro. Really?" Kyle yells in excitement and Trista's eyes grow wide as she screams.

"Mom, are you having a baby?" Josh says pulling out the shirts that say I'm going to be a big brother again and another that says I'm going to be a big sister.

"How about were having two,"

"Twins," Belia shouts looking over at us with a huge grin on her face. "Oh, my gosh congratulations Marissa. She says rushing over to hug me.

The room explodes with laughter, excitement, and a lot of crying as they each take turns coming over to hug us. His mother was overwhelmed with joy that it took her at least 5 minutes to get herself under control. The kids were so excited that they were crying and hugging me so tight telling me they loved me over and over again. After everyone finally calmed themselves we headed into the dining room to have dinner.

233

Chapter Twenty-Five

Brendan

Our parents were overjoyed by the news and the kids were on cloud nine. I don't think they left Marissa's side for the rest of the night. Everyone enjoyed dinner and dessert then we all relaxed in the family room and spent time together talking and playing games. We'd explained to everyone what had happened earlier in the day and that was the reason we were late. I didn't want them to worry or to spoil the surprise of telling them in the way she wanted to unless it was necessary but it all worked out. Once I noticed Marissa getting a little burnt out we said goodnight to the family and I helped her up to bed.

"Thanks, Belia for staying and helping clean up," I said offering her a warm smile.

"Of course, I'm happy to help," she smiles.

We clean up the kitchen and straighten up the rest of the house before I see her out. I get the kids tucked into bed then head into the bedroom to check on Marissa before taking a shower.

"Hey, baby, are you ok?" I say softly.

"I'm fine," she says reaching her arms out to me and I lay across the bed and lift her shirt to kiss her stomach. "You boys gave your dad a good scare today," I say to hear tummy.

"Boys?" She questions

"Yeah, I think we're going to have two rowdy little boys on our hands." I reply.

"And if they're girls?" she asks.

"Well then I guess were going to have to get a couple more tiaras," I wink at her and she laughs running her fingers through my hair.

"I love you," she whispers.

"I love you more," I say leaning in to kiss her.

I head into the bathroom and take a quick shower then climb into bed and cuddle up next to her pulling her in close to me. This feeling that I have right now I never want to lose this every again.

****

When I told everyone the news about Marissa being pregnant with twins everyone in the office was full of congratulations and well wishes. Janice was shocked to hear the news since she is the only one that really knows me best, but she was happy for me. She'd been here through it all and she'd seen me at my worst and now she's happy to see me soaring high and in love. She knew that kids were never really apart of my future plan, but she would always tell me that when the right woman came along all of that would change, and she was right.

The day flew by and I was happy that it has gone by quick and smooth so that I can get out of here and back home to Marissa. Being on bed rest was really getting to her because she's so used to being on the go so having to sitting still for a long period of time is driven her nuts. I get inside, and I check on her then walk her mother out before getting dinner

235

started. I've never really had to do all of this before, but I'll admit I actually love it. Once the food is done I call the kids down and we all sit in the living room and eat dinner since the sofa is a little more comfortable for her.

"How was your day babe?" She asks.

"It was great," I reply with a smile.

"Good," She says, and I notice the weird look on her face.

"What's wrong baby?" I ask, and she lowers her eyes to her plate and begins pushing the food around with her fork. She stays quiet for a second then looks up at me.

"I can't take this anymore," she whispers and I'm guessing it's, so the kids don't hear. "I think I'm going to go insane if I have to go another second with you not touching me Brendan," she says, and I stare at her with wide eyes because I was kind of taking back then I laugh. "Babe it's not funny," she says elbowing me.

"Is that it?" I ask.

"Yes," she sighs.

"Baby Dominic said no strenuous activity,"

"I know—but I'm so freaking horny," she says whispering the last part and I laugh again.

"Mm… so you really want me huh?"

"Stop it," she says squinting at me.

"Oh, no, I want to hear this. I want to hear all about how bad you need me," I reply biting my bottom lip.

"Ok, how about we go up to the room and I can show you," She says leaning in and brushing her tongue across my bottom lip and my dick jumps to attention.

It's been two weeks since we've had sex and honestly, she wasn't the only one feeling the effects of the drought. But I'm not sure it's a good idea for us to engage in anything at the moment even though I want so bad to get her off. Of course, I've handled myself a few times, but I would rather feel the warmth of her wetness sliding up and down my cock.

"I really think that we should wait until after your appointment," I say, and I could see the disappointment in her eyes.

"Ok," She says pouting with her lip poking out and all I could do was shake my head and laugh.

After dinner, I got the kids into bed then headed off to our room to take a quick shower before getting ready for bed.

The hot water running over my body relaxed my muscles and soothed the aching that I felt. I turn off the shower, grab my towel, and drying off before wrapping it around my waist. I figured Marissa would have fallen asleep while I was in the shower, but she was awake and waiting for me when I walked out of the bathroom. A smile spreads across her face and her eyes lower to my towel as soon as I step through the door. I knew exactly what she was thinking, and I shook my head at her, but she ignored me and got up from the bed and walked over to me.

"Marissa, no baby," I say to her stepping back a little.

"Don't worry I have something different in mind," she said taking my hand and pulling me over to the bed.

I sit on the edge of the bed and she drops to her knees pulling off my towel. She smiles up at me when she sees that I'm semi-hard already then takes my dick in her hand and begins to slowly stroke my shaft. She lowers her mouth onto the tip of my head and lets her tongue run over the tip and my dick stiffens in her hand. I let out a low, throaty groan and tilt my head back as she wraps her lips around the head and slowly sucks. The hot, wet, moist feel of her mouth moving up and down my shaft was so intense that my release began to build quickly. I ran my hands through her hair, pushing it out of her face, and gripping it in my fist as her head bobbed up and down. When she glances up at me and winks, it takes everything in me not to bust at the sight of her.

"Get up here," I whisper, and she releases me, stands to her feet, and pulls off her gown before shimming out of her panties.

She climbs up on the bed and straddles my face. The sweet smell of her is so enticing that I couldn't wait for a taste. I part her lips with my tongue then tease her clit with my tongue before sucking on her pearl and feeling her body tremble. She rode my tongue just like she would if it was my dick while she spits, sucks, and slurps on my dick until I couldn't hold back anymore. Once I got her through her second orgasm I couldn't bite back the intense feeling anymore and I shot my load deep into her throat.

"Mm… tasty," She says wiping the come off her face.

"I see you got your way," I smile up at her.

"Don't I always," she says leaning over and kissing me.

"Baby I really need you to take it easy, please." I say sitting up and pulling her onto my lap facing me. "I don't want anything happening to you or our babies."

"I know I just needed to feel you touch me," she said placing her hands on my cheek and kissing me again.

"Such a naughty girl," I say as I shake my head.

After we clean ourselves up we climb into bed and get comfortable making small talk until we doze off to sleep.

****

I was thankful the work day to be over and even more grateful that it's Friday. I decided to go get drinks with Jamison and Kyle this evening after the office closed so that we could catch up. I haven't had much free time lately, so it will be great to have a chance to hang out with the fellas. I change into a pair of jeans, a white crew neck shirt, and grab my leather jacket before leaving the office and heading over to the bar. Driving home to change out of my suit and driving back was going to be a bit much so I brought my clothes to the office.

I arrive at the bar and park curbside and get out of the car. The sun was going down and I could tell from the noise that the bar was already crowded. I catch the eye of two ladies standing by the front entrance as I walk up, and they follow me inside. I go up to the bar and order a beer before turning to skim the place for any signs of the fellas. Neither of them was in the crowded room so I dig my phone out of my pocket and send the both of them a quick text asking where they are. Kyle texts back immediately and says he's five minutes away and a second later a message comes through from Jamison saying he's walking in the door.

I look over to the entrance and see Jamison standing by the door searching them room, so I wave my hand to get his attention. Once he notices me he heads over to the bar to join me.

"What's up man," He says bumping fist with me and taking a seat on the stool to my right. "Sheesh, it's really packed in here tonight." He says looking around the room once more.

"Yeah seems like everyone in town needed to let loose after this work week," I reply.

"Is your brother here yet?" He asks.

"Not yet. But he should be here any minute go ahead and order." I say nodding my head towards the bartender.

Just as I take another sip of my beer I feel a hand grip my biceps and a young, petite woman step in between me and Jamison facing me. She had a smile on her face that could light up a room, brown sugar colored skin, and hair that looked like it was kissed by the sun.

"Well hello handsome," She said leaning against the bar.

"Hello," I say then glance over at Jamison and he looks at me with a smirk on his face.

"You look like you could use a friend," she says running her hand down my arm.

"Uh, actually I'm enjoying my time with the friend sitting behind you," I reply, and she turns and looks at Jamison.

"Oh," she says quickly, and Jamison looks over at her and winks. "I'm sorry I didn't know the two of you were a thing." She says tilting her head to one side.

I chuckle, "No, sweetheart we're not gay it's just that we're both in committed relationships with two gorgeous women." I say.

"Sorry, darling looks like you're going to have to get your nightly dose of cock else were," Jamison smirks and she sucks her teeth before flipping him the finger and walks away.

We both look at each other for a second then laugh before order another beer. Kyle finally joins us, and we grab a table in the back where we could chat until one of the pool tables opened up. We made small talk discussing or plans for the weekend which mainly consisted of spending time with the women in our lives. After about an hour one of the tables opened up and I headed to the front to get us some sticks. Our conversation carried over to the game where we played a couple of games.

The conversations with my friends were so different now. Before we use to talk about sports, work, and exchange stories about how many women we'd bedded by the end of the week. But now all we talk about is relationships, kids, and future plans. Don't get me wrong we love it, but it still amazes me just how much our lives have changed since we meet our women.

Chapter Twenty-Six

Marissa

Today we find out the sex of the babies the kiddos are excited, and so are we. The drive to the hospital was quiet but once we arrived all of the nerves had settled in and I'm not sure why. I mean this pregnancy has sure been a scary one, but I know that the babies are healthy and growing like weeds. I've put on at least ten pounds over the last few months and my doctor says that's a healthy weight gain, but I feel like I weigh a ton. My breast is huge, my thighs have spread, and my ass—my gosh my ass is huge.

"Good Morning Hopkin's family," Dominic says as he enters the room.

"Hello doctor," Jasmine says a bit loudly and he smiles.

"Good Morning Dominic," Brendan says shaking his hand and I say a quick hello after.

"So, let's take a look at the twins and see how things are going shall we,"

I take a deep breath and slowly exhale as I relax back on the exam table. Brendan stands beside me while Josh sits in a chair by the bed and Jasmine sits on the counter so that she's high enough to see the screen. Once he rolls the wand across my tummy the images appear and Jasmine gasps covering her mouth with her hands kicking her little feet. We watch as the images flutter and move while he checks the heart beats and takes down all of the other information he needs.

242

"Alright, babies look great. Make sure that you're continuing to take it easy and eating healthy." He said, "Now are you ready to learn the sex of your twins?"

"YES!" We all say together.

He moves around a little more and for a second, we didn't think that they were going to let the doctor get the images. He stands and shifts my belly around then tries again and this time it worked.

"It looks like you're going to be adding two more boys to the bunch," He says clicking a few buttons on the keypad to take a few pictures.

Tears stream down my cheeks as Brendan leans in and holds me tight. He'd gotten exactly what he wished for twin boys and the look on his face made my heart swell. I didn't really care what the sex of our babies was going to be my only concern is to have two healthy babies come into this loving family. And I will never forget this moment or how it feels to see the excitement on my little one's faces.

We leave the doctors office and head over to the restaurant to grab a bite to eat because the kids and I are starving. I haven't spent much time at the restaurant lately, but I do stop by every now and again and check up with on how things are going. The crowd inside of the restaurant let me know that business was thriving and that my team was doing great with keeping things running well. I head back to my office to talk with Karen while Brendan and the kids are seated by the greeter.

"Omgosh look at you," Karen says as I walk into the office. "You are glowing, what's going on?"

"Thanks, so how's everything going?" I ask slowly lowering myself down into the chair in front of the desk.

"Great, everything's been running smoothly. The numbers are up, and we just had a visit a couple of days ago and we passed with flying colors." She beamed leaning back into her chair.

"That's awesome. It looks like I left the place in the right hands." I reply with a smile.

"You did, and I thank you for entrusting in me the opportunity." She grins.

"Well, the family is waiting for me. I will check back again next week and remember to call me if you need anything." I say as I stand up.

"Don't worry if there is anything I will definitely reach out." She replies walking around the desk then giving me a quick hug.

I join the kids and Brendan back at the table where they were patiently waiting for me to return. I wave to our waitress and she rushes over to take our orders.

"Hey, it's good to see you, Ms. Wilmore. What can I get for you all?"

She takes our orders then heads off to retrieve our drinks and returns a few seconds later. Some people think it's weird to dine at your own restaurant, but I say why the hell not? It's great food, you get to spend time with your family, and you can be a personal taste tester to the in-house chef. I mean what better way to know if your customers are getting the best quality serves and food. When she returns with our food we eat up and make small talk and since the kids were tired we decided to get our dessert to go. I go back and say a quick hello to the chef and the kitchen staff and let them know that they're doing an awesome job then we head home.

****

I started with the plans for our wedding focusing only on the details, location, and décor, since I have to wait until after the twins are born, I'm not going to think about trying on wedding gowns right now. Belia, Trista, and Natalie have been keeping me company while Brendan is working. My mother stops by more than she needs to but then again that's my mother she's always been so overprotective when it comes to her girls.

It took me awhile to figure out how I was going to as the girls to be my bridesmaids, and I wanted to ask my sister in an extra special way to be my maid of honor. So, I browsed the internet until I found the perfect ways then put them into motion. Each of them happily accepted and Natalie was so emotionally overwhelmed that she could barely get a yes out. Now every conversation is filled with questions about the wedding or about the babies. Having babies and planning a wedding so close together is super stressful but I'm thankful to have great friends and family to help me. Brendan has been super sweet and supportive as well. Unlike most men he's actually helped me with deciding on different things for the wedding instead of hitting me with the "Whatever you want babe it's your day," line that pretty much all men say.

After sorting through bridal books and looking through tons of photos online of wedding dresses I decided to take a break. The kids are still at school and the Brendan is at work, so I still have 4 hours before there will be anyone to keep me company. I settle on the couch and put my feet up and

245

picking up the remote to scroll through the guide trying to find something to watch. The only thing on during this time of day is daytime talk shows and reruns of reality shows. I come across an old movie and settle on that after a while simply because I didn't want to continue looking.

It didn't take long for me to begin to doze off only a few minutes seeing as to how that is usually the outcome nowadays. I'm always tired and if I sit for more then a couple of minutes I'm watching the back of my eyelids.

A sharp pain shoots through my stomach and it startles me awake I sit up quickly and place my hands on my belly. The pain subsides after a few seconds and I relax back on the couch taking slow and steady breaths. I think perhaps today I've been on my feet a little much and I think to myself that tomorrow I'm going to spend most of my day sitting very still. But as soon as I relax another sharp pain shots through my stomach and I sit up once more.

"Ah..." I scream as I reach for my phone.

I unlock my phone and press Brendan's name and place the phone to my ear. It rings several times but no answer, so I hang up and redial the number again. After another series of rings, the voicemail comes over the line again. I pull up Natalie's number and press dial, she picks up on the second ring.

"What's up, sis?" She asks in a cheery voice.

"Nat help," I say my voice barely a whisper.

"Marissa, are you there, what's wrong?" She asks her voice high pitched.

"Ah—" I scream into the phone. "Nat help me it hurts so bad," I say in between screams.

"Omgosh Marissa," She shouts, "I'm on my way just hold on."

I hang up and try calling my mother and she answers on the first ring. I'm guessing that Natalie called her a soon as we hung because my mother shouts into the phone that she's on her way as soon as she picks up. I try to stay calm and not panic but home alone and the level of pain that I was feeling was freaking me the fuck out. I've birthed two children, and never once did I feel the type of pain that I'm feeling at this very moment which was freaking me out even more.

I hear the door open and then I see Natalie's belly come around the corner. She was almost as huge as mean and she was only caring one child. My mother came around the corner behind her and they both rushed over to me.

"Can you stand up sweetheart?" My mother asks, and I shake my head yes instead of speaking so that I could focus on my breathing.

"Can someone please call Brendan," I say as I try to get up from the couch which was a failed attempt I might add.

"Oh no, take it easy Marissa," Natalie says. "Wait just sit still I'm going to have Kolby carry you to the car."

"Kolby?" I ask with a questioning look on my face.

"Yes, Kolby," she smiles then heads back towards the front door.

I look at my mom and she gives me that 'don't ask' look so I let it go. A second later Kolby comes walking inside and oh boy had he grown up he looked so different. If she hadn't already told me it was him I might not of none who he was. He smiles and says hello as he scoops me up off the couch and into his arms. He was cut, shoulders broad, and his arms were muscular. He carried me out to the car with ease and placed me in the back seat climbing in behind me while my mom got in the front and Nat in the driver's seat.

"Holy fuck," I scream out and Kolby turns quickly to me.

"Are you ok," he asks, and I give him a venomous look. "I'm sorry of course you're not ok." He says.

We pull into the hospital and he helps me out of the car once more carrying me inside as Natalie followed along. My mother calls out to us telling us that she'll meet us after she parks the car. The pain was getting stronger and the contractions closer together.

"Um, Marissa, did you just use the bathroom," Kolby asks.

"Oh gosh, my water just broke," I say looking up at him.

"Here put her in the wheelchair," Natalie says and slowly sits me in the seat.

We hurry upstairs, and the nurse sees us as we enter and rushes over to us asking how she could help and I shout for her to get these babies out of me. Knowing exactly what that meant she rushed us to a room and called for my doctor.

"Nat, did you get a hold of Brendan," I ask.

"Mom is still trying to get him but don't worry." She replies.

My mom comes bursting through the door just as my sister finishes up and lets me know that Brendan is on his way. A wave of relief washes over me and I feel a little calmer that is until the next contraction ripped through me. I couldn't help but wonder why I was going in to labor so soon and I was so scared that it was something that I'd done. I'm only seven months and two weeks so why are the babies coming now. The nurse returns and checks my cervix to see how far I've dilated before letting me know that I was four centimeters'.

"Ms. Wilmore, I didn't expect to see you here for another couple of months," Dominic jokes as he walks into the room.

"I didn't plan to see you so soon either doc," I say with a weak smile.

"Well let's take a look shall we," He says placing a glove on his hand and checking my cervix once again. "Six centimeters, you seem to be dilating quickly. I think well be ready to push in just a few. Now I didn't go over how you would like to during your delivery, but we can do that now, would you like to be medicated, Ms. Wilmore?"

"Yes," I shout and everyone in the room gives a small chuckle.

"Alright, the nurse will prep you for an epidural and I'll be back shortly.

He leaves the room and Brendan comes in just as he is leaving. I've never been so relieved in my life I was happy to see him walking through the door.

"I'm sorry baby I was with a patient and my phone was in my office," he says as he comes over and kisses.

A different nurse comes into the room and asks everyone to step out except Brendan so that she could prep me for my epidural. Natalie and my mom give me a quick kiss and a hug then go out to the waiting room with Kolby trailing behind them. I'd opted out of getting them with my previous pregnancy but with the pains that I'm feeling I don't think I'll make it through this one. Especially with two babies exiting my body just the thought of it all made me fill a bit woozy. Five minutes later the epidural was in and I could immediately feel the pain subsiding and I could finally relax.

By this time my father and his parents had arrived and came into the room to greet us. Both of our mother's and Natalie decided to be in the room during the birth but not the men. It wasn't something that they wanted to experience again. When it was time for me to push everyone exited the room and Dominic returned and took his place at the foot of the bed.

Chapter Twenty-Seven

Brendan

I couldn't believe that I'd missed all those calls from Marissa and when I got the message from her mom I panicked. But once I arrived and I saw her face all of those fears washed away. Even though I was still a little worried about the babies coming early I was eager to meet the little guys. As Dominic instructs her to push I hold tight to her hand allowing her to squeeze as hard as she needs to through each contraction. I actually expected to be squeamish and freaked out by the site of it all, but it was beautiful and so was she.

"You got this baby, just one more push," I say rubbing her shoulder.

"The first baby is almost here," Dominic shouts.

Marissa takes a deep breath then pushes one last time and we hear aloud squeal. Baby A had made his entrance into the world and with a healthy set of pipes on him as well. Dominic gives her a second to relax than as soon as the next contraction comes we begin again. After a good three pushes baby B makes his way out and squeals just as loud as his brother. Happy tears flowed from everyone in the room.

"You did great baby," I say and kiss her on the top of her head as she sobs into my chest.

I hold her close and stroke her hair until the nurse comes over with our first son and hands him to Marissa. A couple of seconds later another nurse comes over with our other son and places him in my arms.

"Congratulations you two," Dominic says giving us a nod. "I'll be back to check on you in the morning Marissa." He says before leaving the room.

I stare down at this tiny little human that we've created and brought into the world. The feeling that's come with holding my very first child has taken first place in everything in my life. There is no greater feeling in the world than looking into the eyes of your own flesh and blood. I hand him to Marissa so that she could have some time with them both together before they take them away to the nursery. The look in her eyes was the same look she gives when she's looking at Josh and Jasmine. The love, happiness, and pure joy that oozes out of her is contagious and I knew that she was going to give all of that and more to our boys.

Natalie and Mrs. Wilmore hug me then go out to the waiting room to tell the rest of the family that the babies have arrived and that they're healthy baby boys. After Marissa gets cleaned up and changed into a fresh gown, we head over to the room she'll be in for the remainder of her stay. As we enter she gets teary-eyed seeing all of the balloons and flowers that were waiting for her, along with a huge banner on the wall welcoming the twins.

"Omgosh… you guys this is so sweet of you," She says wiping her tears away.

"I'm so happy for the two of you and the twins are adorable," Belia says walking over and hugging her.

"Thank you," Marissa says with a soft smile.

I roll her chair up to the bed, help up, and then into the bed. She settles in and gets comfortable and we continue to talk and visit with the family until the nurse returns with the twins. We hadn't really made a final decision on the boy's names simply because we thought we'd have plenty of time to find the perfect names. Marissa chose to breastfeed, so once the babies returned, everyone said their goodbyes then made their exit for the night. I didn't realize how exhausted I was until I actually took a second to sit down and relax.

"How are you feeling baby?" I ask offering her a smile.

"I'm fine, but you look tired. Maybe you should take a nap." She replies.

"I'm ok," I say, and she raises her brow making me chuckle. "I promise I'm good."

"Brendan, you need to rest. Come and lie down please." She says with the cutest pouty face I've ever seen so I couldn't argue with that.

I get up and crawl into the bed beside her resting my head on the pillow watching as she nursed our son. The room light wakes me, and I blink my eyes a couple of times before turning on my side searching around the room. I didn't remember falling asleep, I was slightly dazed and couldn't remember where I was.

"Mr. Hopkins, are you ok?" The nurse asks resting her hand on my shoulder.

"Uh, yeah," I say clearing my throat and sitting up on the bed. "I kind of forgot where I was. Is everything ok?"

"Yes sir, I'm just here to check on your wife and give her, her meds."

"Where is she?" I ask looking to my left.

"She's in the bathroom." She says, and I smile giving her a quick nod before getting up from the bed and walking over to the bathroom.

I knock on the door twice two small knocks, "Are you ok baby?"

"Yes, I'll be out in second," Marissa says.

I go back over to the bed and take my seat on the edge rubbing the sleep from my eyes and placing my head in my arms. As soon as I hear the bathroom door open I rush over to help her back to the bed.

"I'm ok Brendan," she giggles.

I take her hand from the nurse that was inside helping her and said a quick thank you before placing her arm around mine and walking her over to the bed. She sits on the edge before swinging her legs onto the bed and sliding back. I grab my bag and head to the bathroom to change into a pair of sweatpants and a crew neck t-shirt. When I come out of the bathroom, the nurse had just finished giving Marissa her medicine and glanced up at me freezing mid-step as she looked me over.

"He's quite yummy isn't he," she giggles, and the nurse face turns a bright shade of red as her eyes lower to the floor.

"I'm so sorry," she murmurs embarrassment staining her face.

"Don't be," Marissa replies, and the nurse gives her a nervous smile before exiting the room. "You're going to be someone's wet dream tonight." She jokes, and I shake my head as I slide into the bed and lean in kissing her lips softly.

****

I rock gently from side to side trying to soothe my fussy son. I can tell that he's going to be the one with the most character.

"You know we should really pick out names," I say to Marissa as she nurses the other twin.

"I know," She replies. "How about you give them their names. These are your first-born sons, so I think you should have the pleasure of naming." She says with a smile.

"Really?" I ask, and she shakes her head.

I turn back to the window and let my mind drift off as I think of the perfect names. I know that most fathers usually names picked out or at least have some sort of idea of what they want to name their firstborn. But for me, I never really imagined myself in this position, so I've actually never thought about. I do however want to give them names that they'll be proud of when they are older.

"What do you think about the names Malik and Makah Hopkins?" I say turning back towards her and her face lights up as our eyes connect.

"I love it," She says softly, and I can't help but return the smile.

"Malik and Makah," I said staring down at my son. "Yeah, that's perfect."

A knock on the door breaks my concentration and I turn to look at the door and see Dominic walk into the room giving me a quick nod before walking over to Marissa.

"How are we doing this morning Ms. Wilmore?" He asks stepping over to the computer and powering it up.

"I'm doing fairly well," She replies with a warm smile.

I take Malik and lay him in his bed before going over and taking Makah from Marissa and lying him in his bed. Dominic spends the next five minutes asking Marissa a few questions before giving her a quick exam. He lets us know that if everything continues to go well that she'll be able to go home in a couple of days. It's a miracle that the twins are healthy and doing as well as they are especially arriving a month and a half early.

Our family arrives around noon and the kids were excited to get to meet their baby brothers for the first time. Jasmine was the first to hold the babies because as she states she's the big sister and she's a princess, so she goes first. I sit back and watch as everyone moves around the room and can't help but to feel grateful for every single person in the room. My family!

Chapter Twenty-Eight

Marissa

The overwhelming feeling of pure joy and excitement that filled me when the nurse placed my baby boys in my arms will forever be etched into my memory. The look on Brendan's face brought tears to my eyes and having my sister and my mother here to share this moment with me was picture perfect. I'm happy with how well Brendan has handled everything and I love how protective he is of me. I was a little worried about the babies being born so early and I was scared that they were going to have to stay in the NICU. But they came into the world healthy and absolutely perfect.

After the nurse took them to the nursery for the night, I watched Brendan as he slept. I can't believe that this beautiful human being chose me and that we are parents to two healthy twins, Malik and Makah. I can't help but say their names over and over again. The names are perfect, and I couldn't think of anything better. I knew that he would come up with the perfect names, and I knew that it would be perfect for them to be named by their father.

I was happy to hear that I would be able to go home in just a couple of days. Because regardless of what most people think the hospital is definitely not a place for privacy or rest. Plus, I miss being in my own bed and having alone time with Brendan.

"Hello Ms. Wilmore, how are you feeling?"

"A little sore," I reply.

"Would you like something for that." She asks.

"Yes, please."

"I'll go and grab you something I'll be right back." She says before putting a few more things into the computer then heads out the room.

She returns a few minutes later with some pain relievers. After I take the pills they begin to kick in rather quickly and I doze off.

****

It felt great to have everything back to normal and be able to get back to the restaurant. I really missed being here and I missed seeing my employees as well, although I knew it was in great hands, I still missed the day to day hustle and bustle of it all. I was back to doing what I love and finishing up the final touches on my plans for the wedding. My whole family has been a big help when it comes to the kids and helping me, and Brendan maintains balance.

Our parent's alternate weekends so that Brendan and I get a break. Natalie also babysits as well so that we can squeeze in a date night every now and again. Kolby and Natalie decided to rekindle their relationship and they seem to be happy. Natalie gave birth to my beautiful niece a month after the twins were born and Kolby proposed to her at the hospital a couple of days after the birth. I'm proud of my sister and the growth she's shown since having her daughter. Becoming a mother and finding love again has helped heal a lot of old wounds helping her to move forward.

And speaking of date nights, I need to get my work done so that I can get home and get ready for tonight's. I head back to my office and finish up the pile of paperwork that has been sitting on my desk for most of the week. I try and breeze through them quickly as possible to ensure that I'm not late, just as I close the book there's a knock on the door.

"Hey, Marissa, there is a young guy in the front asking for you," Karen says poking her head in the door.

I grab my jacket and my purse and head out to the front to see who it was. When I walk around the corner, I see the tall slender guy smiling at me from the doorway and I wave to him.

"Hello Ahmad," I say walking over and giving him a warm embrace. "What are you doing here?"

"Mr. Hopkins requested that I pick you up this evening," He says.

"Oh, did he, now," I say with a smirk and he laughs. "Well, let's not keep Dr. Hopkins waiting," I say with a wink then head to towards the front door.

He turns on his heels and quickly rushes over to the door and opens it for me. Once we get to the car he opens the door and I climb inside. Several minutes later we pull up to the Boutique Shop that Ahmad brought me to the night of the Awards ceremony for Brendan.

"Ahmad, what's going on?" I ask curiosity ringing in my tone.

"This is our first stop."

He steps out of the car and comes around to open my door. I take his hand and he assists me out of the care and up to the front pulling it open for me and holding his hand out

259

ushering me inside. I turn and smile at her before placing a kiss on his cheek then I head inside. The same young lady was waiting for me when I entered the store, she greeted me then showed me to the back.

When I get to the back I find my mother, Mrs. Hopkins, Natalie, Jasmine, Belia, and Trista waiting for me. I look around the room at everyone trying to figure out just what they are up to now because I'm sure that Brendan has cooked up some grand plan to surprise me somehow.

"What's going on you guys?" I smile.

"Oh, you'll see," Natalie says grinning from ear to ear.

The young redhead returns with something in her hand and hangs it on the hook over the dressing room behind my mother and my sister then leaves the room. Natalie turns and removes the covering then steps to the side and there it was my perfect dress. The Princess V-Neck Sweep Train Tulle Wedding Dress hung on display and I gaze at it in awe as tears stung my eyes.

"Well don't just stand there crying go in and try it on." My mother says.

Natalie helps me into the dress than I go back out into the room to take a look in the mirror.

"Perfection," I whisper to myself as I take in this beautiful masterpiece that clings to my every curve. Every stitch, every diamond, every single detail is exactly the way that I wanted it to be.

"You look amazing, sis," Natalie says with tears streaming from her eyes.

There wasn't a dry eye in the room, and when I turn to speak to everyone I see my bridesmaids standing behind me in their dresses and my beautiful daughter in hers as well and I completely and utterly break down.

"Come on sweetheart dry your tears because we're not quite finished." She says taking my arm and leading me out of the room and into the salon where a hair and make-up team are waiting.

I sit down in the seat and before my tush could get comfortable in the seat the team got to work. An hour and a half later my full make-up and hair were complete, and it was done exactly the way I'd imagined it for my wedding day. I headed back to the dressing room and put on my dress then I as lead out to the car where Ahmad was still parked in the same spot waiting for me. I smile up at him then climb into the car taking my seat as he goes around to the driver side and takes his seat. He pulls away from the shop and heads off to the next surprise destination.

My palms were getting sweaty and my heart begins to race as I begin to realize just what this was that he'd planned. Ahmad helps me out of the car and walks me down the long sidewalk and up to the gate that leads to the garden at our home where I'd planned to have our wedding. A small intimate wedding while the sunsets has always been the wedding I'd dreamed of since I was young. But when Chandler and I got married we were young and didn't have the means to have the kind of wedding I'd dreamed of. Nonetheless, I was happy with the wedding that we had.

We reach the entrance and my father is waiting for me by the water fountain. He looks so handsome in his grey tux and the expression on his face made my eyes fill with tears, but I quickly blink them away not wanting to ruin my make-up. I take a deep breath and Ahmad releases my arm and I walk over to my father and take his hand. He pulls me into a hug and kisses me on the cheek.

"You look beautiful, sweetheart,"

"Thank you, daddy," I say returning a kiss to his cheek.

He takes my arm into his and I hear the soft music begins to play and the gates to the entrance slowly open. Jasmine walks up beside me and wraps her arms around my waist and squeezes me tight.

"You look really pretty mommy," she says smiling up at me.

"Thank you, baby," I said offering her a warm smile leaning down and kissing her on the cheek.

Ahmad ushers her towards the door then she steps towards the entrance and slowly walks inside throwing flowers at her feet with each step. My father and I step inside and I see Brendan standing a few feet away from me smiling and my body relaxes. My lips spread into the widest grin that I've ever had in my life and our eyes connect. Every person and every sound in the room was gone and there was no one else there but me and him. He looked so good in his tailored tux that hugged each and every muscle on his body in the most exquisite way. Thoughts rushed my mind and I pictured removing each and every layer off him before making love to him tonight.

"Sweetheart," my father whispers in my ear pulling me from my thoughts.

We'd made it to the front and I hadn't realized, I stretch out my hand and place it into his and he helps me up onto the

262

stairs. The minister asks everyone to take their seats and the ceremony begins. We agreed to say our own vows and I wanted it to be that way because I feel like saying your own vows is way more intimate and makes the moment that much more special.

"I now pronounce you Mr. and Mrs. Hopkins. Brendan, you may kiss your bride."

He places his hands on each side of my face and pulls me into the most electrifying kiss that we've ever shared. I'm not sure how long that we were caught in the moment, but the sounds of our guest pulled us out once we realized them. When we turn to face our guest, everyone claps and cheers as we make our way down the aisle.

He leads me into the house and into his study closing the door behind me after I walk in.

"Brendan, baby I can't believe you did all of this—" I begin saying and he comes over to me quickly pulling me into his arms as his lips crash into mine. He kisses me feverishly, his hands roaming aimlessly over my body gripping me in all the right places. I put my arms around his neck and place my hands at the nape of his neck pulling him deeper into the kiss and he lifts me up and sits me on the desk.

"You look so fucking sexy," he says in between kisses and a moan escapes me as he trails little kiss down my neck letting his tongue brush my collarbone.

"Brendan we can't," I say, and he looks up at me with his dark lust filled eyes and pushes my lace panties to the side and slowly pushes his fingers inside of me.

My breath catches in my throat as the pleasure builds inside of me. He continues to watch me biting his bottom lip as he moves his figures in and out of me vigorously. The way that he's looking at me and the way that his fingers are working my insides while his thumb teases my clit sends me over the edge quickly. My body trembles and shakes as I tilt my head back and close my eyes as a mind-blowing orgasm rips through me like a volcano erupting.

"Omgosh…" I shout as I find my voice.

"That's right baby come for me," he says as his fingers continue there play until my orgasm runs its course.

He leans in and kisses me on the lips then pulls away smiling as he turns and walks over to the corner of the office and grabs a towel from one of the drawer. He goes into the bathroom and comes back over to me handing me the damp towel. I take it from him and clean myself before straightening my dress back out.

"I just couldn't resist," he says kissing me on the cheek.

"You're such a bad boy," I say getting down from the desk and tugging on his jacket pulling him closer. I run my tongue over his bottom lip then place a kiss in the same spot.

He chuckles, "I'll show you just how bad tonight," he smirks.

"You promise," I whisper into his ear letting my tongue brush over the spot just under his ear and he lets his hand wander down to my ass and gives it a good smack and I yelp then laugh. "Come on let's get back out there."

I take my hand and I follow him out of the office and out to the back of the house where a huge tent was set up, and everyone was waiting patiently for us to arrive. Music is

264

playing, and I can see everyone slowly rocking from side to side enjoying themselves.

"Wait," I say to him pulling his hand back and he stops and looks at me.

"What is it?" He asks.

"Thank you," I respond.

"For?"

"All of this," I say waving my hand in the air. "Thank you for loving my kids and I, thank you for letting us into your heart and always putting us first. Thank you for our beautiful twins and thank you a million times over for giving me my dream wedding." I say stepping closer to him as he puts his arms around my waist.

"It's my pleasure, Mrs. Hopkins," he smiles. "I plan to spoil you and our children for the rest of our lives, you all are the best thing that's happened in my life."

"I look forward to that and so much more."

"I love you."

"I love you more, Mr. Hopkins."

Epilogue

Brendan

"Babe can you grab the twins," Marissa shouts down to me from the hall.

I chase down the twins and carry them to their room to get them dressed for their brother's graduation. It's been ten years since Marissa and I married and we're still happily going strong. The twins have grown, and man they sure are a handful, Jasmine is maturing into a beautiful, smart, and respectful teen, and Josh is graduating from high school today or, so we hope. If I don't get these boys to settle down and get them dressed he just might miss the ceremony.

"Dad we're going to be late," Josh shouts up the stairs. "Mom are you even ready yet?"

"Calm down I'm almost finished," Marissa says walking past the room towards the stairs.

I rush downstairs with the boys on either side of my arms and set them down when I reach the last stair. We head out to the car, quickly get inside, and head over to the high school. Josh hops out the car and kisses his mother through the window then waves to me telling us that he'll see us inside before running into the building.

Once we park the car we go inside with just five minutes to spare, and it takes all of that to find the rest of the family. I'm happy they saved us seats in the front because every seat here is filled, it looks to me like the whole town is here. We listen

266

to the speeches then watch as each student goes up to collect their diploma's. We'd told Josh that we would behave and not make a big scene but when his name was called we were all so excited and happy that we were up out of our seats and cheering for him.

We wait for him in the parking lot while everyone else heads to the restaurant to prepare for the surprise for Josh and his friends. Marissa and a few of the other mothers got together and planned a graduation party for Josh and his classmates.

"I'm so proud of you son," Marissa says as he walks up to and into her embrace.

"Thanks, mom," He replies kissing her cheek.

"I'm proud of you too," I say giving him a heartfelt embrace.

"Thanks, dad," he says with a grin.

We all climb into the car and pull away, once we arrive at the restaurant I go around, and open Marissa's door. She steps out taking Josh's hand and he places her arm around his. They walk to the door and I follow a couple of steps behind then we all go in. The rest of his friends are waiting at the entrance as we walk up, Marissa had her staff blackout the windows on the door so that no one could see inside. I walk over to the door and Marissa nods to me and I open the door and we walk into the dim lit room and as the lights turn on the crowd yells "SURPRISE," startling them a little. As soon as they noticed their friends and family and all of the decorations they then realized what was going on and Josh turns to hug his mother than me with a huge smile on his face.

The music begins and we all enjoy an even full of dancing, singing, good food, and mingling with family and friends. Josh and his girlfriend present each other with a special gift then his mother and I give him our graduation gift. He's decided to study medicine at one of the world's most prestigious schools, so he'll be heading off to Maryland this fall. We know that he'll be a great surgeon and his mother, and I couldn't be prouder of him and look forward to so many more accomplishments from him.

I think the kids will miss him being around the house, but I know that they are proud of their big brother as well. Marissa has branched out and opened two more restaurants' in Nashville and one in Georgia. My practice is doing well, and I plan on starting another that I will have Jamison head up now that he and Trista are planning to relocate. Life is great and I'm the happiest I've ever been in my entire life, I feel complete.

Marissa

Ten years have now passed, and we are still going strong. I never imagined in my wildest dreams that I would overcome losing the love of my life or that I would ever fall in love again. But here I am, happy, and filled with joy and hope, even right now, at this very moment. We now have four beautiful children that we absolutely love and adore. My career has flourished, and we've opened two more restaurants. On top of all that my son graduated from high school yesterday. He's turned out to be a very smart and handsome young man, and as for my husband he's living his dream as well and making plans to expand and open another practice which will be outside of Nashville. Also, my ever so sweet princess Jasmine is blossoming into a gorgeous, smart, and talented teen.

Today Brendan and I are taking Josh to do a little shopping. In a few weeks, he will be heading off to college to study medicine, I'd noticed years ago that he was interested in what Brendan was doing but I never realized how much. When he told me that he wanted to study to become a surgeon I was shocked but also thrilled at the same time. He's smart so I know that he will accomplish anything that he puts his mind to and he's going to make an excellent surgeon.

We stop by the furniture store first so that he can pick out some new things for his apartment in Maryland.

"So, Josh, what look are you going for?" I ask taking his arm in mine walking alongside him while Brendan walks on my other side.

"I don't know mom," He said, "You know I really want to use the extra room as a study and make it kind of like a really Zen type of area."

"Mm… that sounds like an excellent idea," I said patting him on the arm. "But what will you do if you find a roommate?" I ask, and he stops.

"Yeah…about that mom I need to talk to you and dad about something."

"Um—ok," I say releasing his arm and looking over at Brendan.

"What is it, son?" Brendan asks.

"Maybe we should finish shopping and talk about it over lunch." He says with a nervous expression on his face.

Just as I open my mouth to press the issue Brendan cuts in before I could speak. "Right, let's finish up here and talk about it later." He says with a smile then places his hand on the small of my back, and I nod my head, pull his arm back around mine, and smile up at him. We move around the store with ease as I help him pick out pieces for each room even though Brendan's suggestions are the ones he went for. Once we paid for all the items we left the store and headed to grab lunch and talk.

Josh explained to us that he and his girlfriend were planning to share his apartment, but he wanted to discuss it with us first. I don't really think that it's a good idea for them to move in together at this particular time because I feel as though it's a distraction, but Brendan thinks that it will be good for them. Then I began to think back to when Chandler and I were in college and how we would spend more time at one another's place and less at our own, and after a while it really became pointless to have two separate places. So, I told him that if it's really what they want then they should go for it. I want him to make his own decision so that he can also make mistakes and learn from them rather than try and save him from every situation. He's going out on his own and as scary as that maybe I know that he'll be just fine because he's always been a thinker and a planner. He's also very good at making smart choices so he'll be just fine, I do believe we've raised him well.

We head home and grab the kids so that we can meet up with Natalie, Kolby, and my beautiful niece. The kids have been begging us to see a movie, so we decided to all get-together and have a little family outing.

Nat and I go and grab the popcorn and snacks while our husbands take the kids to the theater and find us some good seats.

Natalie and Kolby got married a year after Brendan and me and they've been happily married ever since. I've never seen my sister smiling and enjoying life as much as I have over the past several years, and I know it's because the love of her life found his way back to her.

It's like my mother always said, "True love will always find it's way back to you. No matter the distance or the time, if it's meant to be it will be."

Acknowledgements

I'm so excited to have finished my second novel and even more excited to share it with you all. I want to thank everyone that helped me in getting this work of art completed, and to my husband for keeping me grounded and focused. Thanks again to my good friend Mark Golson, for continuing to be an amazing set of eyes and for always keeping me on my toes. To my readers thank you, thank you, a million times thank you. You guys are so awesome, and I appreciate each and every one of you. Because of you, I have the chance to live out my dream. Much Love!

Follow Nae T. Bloss

Website:

www.naetblossauthor.com

Facebook:

@AuthorNaeTBloss

Twitter:

@NaeTBloss

Instagram:

@naetblossauthor

If you like what you've read, please leave me a review and let me know.

About the Author

Author, Wife, and Mother to five awesome kiddos! My top three favorite things are books, chocolate, and good music. I've always been passionate about storytelling and impressed by the influence it has on people and the decisions they make in life. As an author I want my readers to get lost in the stories, connect with the characters, and use them as an escape or even a small break from their everyday lives. I've always loved writing poetry, I love writing short stories, and now I can add writing novels to my list of loves.

Up Next

Dream Series

MY DREAM MAN (BOOK 1) **Available Now**

A FORBIDDEN DREAM (BOOK 2)

MY DREAM ENDING (BOOK 3)

COMING SOON

THE UNDERLINED GAME (BOOK 1)

A NEW BEGINNING

BEFRIENDED